SABOTAGE

C. G. COOPER

"SABOTAGE"

A Corps Justice Novel
Copyright © 2016, 2018 C. G. Cooper. All Rights Reserved
Author: C. G. Cooper
Editors: Andrea Kerr & Cheryl Hopton

**GET A FREE COPY OF THE CORPS JUSTICE PREQUEL
SHORT STORY, *GOD-SPEED*, JUST FOR SUBSCRIBING AT
CG-COOPER.COM**

To my faithful readers: thank you for allowing me to continue this awesome writing journey. I could not do this without you.

- CGC

CHAPTER ONE

At the moment, Vince Sweeney looked nothing like an army colonel from the 1st Special Forces Operational Detachment-Delta (Delta Force). Reclining happily in a pristine white leather chair, he wore what he now considered his business attire: khaki cargo shorts, an obnoxious Hawaiian shirt, and Timberland boots. His gnarled hand moved from a glass of whiskey and scratched his scraggly white beard. He'd gone gray early, but had never much bought into a normal man's vanity. With what he did for a living, it helped provide a perfect disguise, when needed. Since his current "job" was almost over, the beard would soon have to go.

As he closed his eyes and relished the cool breeze blowing from the air conditioning vent, he smiled at the thought of going home. How many times had he left? He'd have to go back through his military records to check, not that the records were complete. Being part of Delta Force meant that most operations weren't even classified, thus they were rarely documented. The operations just didn't exist, on paper.

He'd just turned fifty and, because he continuously opted

to stay in the field, refusing to play the game of *Army career-building Monopoly*, he'd be out soon—involuntarily retired. He didn't mind. He'd had a great career, led honest and courageous men and saved countless lives. So, as he took another sip of his well-deserved drink, Colonel Vince Sweeney was content.

"Hey, you gonna drink all that, or are you gonna save some for me?" The man sitting across from him in a nearly identical outfit growled with mock indignation.

Sweeney had known Karl Schneider for just under twenty years. They served together in Delta Force on and off throughout their careers. Although Karl looked like a washed-up bartender with one foot in the grave, he still was one of the toughest men Vince Sweeney had ever met. Karl could take on a man three times his size and win. It probably had something to do with his upbringing. His father had been a coal miner in West Virginia, and prior to enlisting in the army, Karl had worked in the mines for two hard years. That did something to a man, and as the senior enlisted soldier under his command, Karl was not only a superb fighter, but also Colonel Vince Sweeney's best friend.

Vince passed the bottle of Johnnie Walker Black to Karl after he refilled his own glass.

"Did you take a look at those listings I sent you?" Karl asked, handing the bottle back to Sweeney.

"Yeah, I like that place with the little red roof. Looks like something out of a painting my grandma had hanging in her guest bedroom."

Karl nodded appreciatively, equally at the whiskey and Sweeney's choice.

"You know what, Vince? You're not much to look at, but I'd say you're a pretty good judge of real estate."

Karl was on his way out too. He had a couple years on Sweeney which had forced the army to take out its big, fat magnifying glass and give Karl the old up-and-down. Vince knew what the higher-ups were thinking; they had two washed-up soldiers ready to send out to pasture. Never mind the fact that they were Delta warriors. There was always a need to make space for the up-and-comers. Although Vince understood this fact, he was sadder for his friend than for himself.

While the Army, and Delta Force, had been good to Colonel Vince Sweeney, it had been the blood coursing through Karl's veins for thirty years. However, the blood transfusion was about to be taken away. Thus, the two men had made a pact. When they got out and retired for good, they'd leave together. Neither man was married now, though both had each been previously: Vince once and Karl twice. Now neither had any prospects on the horizon, and that was okay with them.

Karl had concocted a plan. They planned to do what a lot of the guys were doing - get out and set up shop on the civilian side. They had plenty of contacts, both active duty military and police forces, all more than willing to utilize their assistance and training. Besides, they each had enough money put away to last them for years; they'd been smart with their finances. Even if no jobs came their way, they'd be more than content living the simple life of hunting in the mornings, strolling to the lake to fish, and growing old together on rickety rocking chairs under that little red roof.

"Yeah." Vince reflected, "That sounds fine. Damn fine."

This journey home was one step closer to that goal.

"You know, I bet if we wait a couple months we might be able to get that place for a steal. It's been on the market for over a year, and the agent said the owners are ready to sell. What do you think, Vince?"

Vince looked over at his friend and smiled.

"I say why wait? Let's do it."

Karl grinned and held out his glass.

"Here's mud in your eye, Vince."

They clinked their glasses and downed the rest of their drinks.

And just like that the conversation was over. It was back to business.

"What do you think the big man's going to say about what we saw?" Karl asked.

Vince shook his head. "I know what he'll say, but it's what he'll do I'm most worried about."

Their current mission came straight from the top. As two of the most seasoned veterans of the famed Delta Force, Karl and Vince were given first shot at the assignment. It didn't hurt that they had a personal reputation with the president of the United States. When he called them, they were only too happy to serve. Besides, masquerading as oil venture entrepreneurs wasn't such a bad gig. Yeah, Africa was hot as hell, but flying first class wasn't too bad, and the mission was important too. Why say no?

Vince and Karl understood the consequences. They'd seen firsthand the developments that the world wasn't supposed to know about. So while Vince was anxious to get home and take his first hot shower in a week, he knew an uncomfortable conversation was coming. Decisions would have to be made, contingencies planned, but that was still hours away. As he and Karl had for years, they would enjoy their current time in the sun. It wasn't every day that you were the only passengers on a swanky private luxury jet, and that's what made the next moment so surreal.

They had only been in the air for thirty minutes when a concussive blast rocked the small airplane. Years of reflexive action and physical memory imprinted on their DNA, now saved both Karl's and Vince's lives. Their seatbelts had been unbuckled, but they clutched onto their chairs for dear life.

There was the sucking wind. At the plane's tail, Vince saw there was a gaping hole four rows back. He saw something fly through the hole and, for the briefest instance, he thought it was Karl. However, when he looked across the aisle Karl had assumed the same position as Vince.

The plane veered off course as the wind tore through the passenger compartment. Vince could barely hear the blaring of the emergency sirens overhead. No one came out of the cockpit, and that was probably for the best. It was sealed, and it was the safest place for the pilots attempting to fly the doomed bus. Neither Vince nor Karl had parachutes or even weapons at their disposal, thus jumping from the plane was ruled out as an option. Instead, with grim nods, the two men climbed back into their chairs and strapped themselves in. *It was going to be one helluva bumpy ride,* Vince and Karl thought to themselves.

————

The pilot was good, really good. He'd somehow manhandled the nosediving aircraft to a safe and secure landing just beyond the edge of some storm-engorged lake. As Vince stepped outside, shielding his eyes from the scorching sun, he smelled leaking fuel. However, Lady Luck was smiling down on them because there weren't any flames. After he performing a quick inspection of the hull's exterior, the only apparent damage was the jagged tear along the aircraft's left side.

Both pilots climbed out of the plane into the bright sunlight. One held onto Karl's arm for support. Neither man appeared injured, but both were visibly shaken, and at first glance, they looked to be in shock.

"Well that's number three for you," Karl said, pointing a

finger at Vince. "Remind me to book a plane home without you on it."

Karl smirked, but the joke was lost on the two pilots, who were looking at their surroundings as if they'd just landed on the moon.

"You two okay?" Vince inquired.

First one pilot and then the other nodded, dazed.

"That was some amazing flying," Vince said with gratitude. "Thank you both. You saved our lives."

The comment did little to shake either pilot from his stupor. It appeared they were in mild shock, which Vince had seen many times before. It was not the debilitating type. They just needed a couple of minutes and water.

"Karl, why don't you go see if the stewardess can bring some water for the gentlemen first, please."

Karl shook his head in dismay. "She's not in there, Vince; I think she got sucked out of the plane. I'll go get some water."

One dead. That poor girl. She'd probably been on her way to see if they needed anything when it all happened. Couldn't do anything about that now.

"Did you call for help?" Vince asked the lead pilot.

The man looked confused, stunned even. Then he shook his head in dismay.

"It was the strangest thing," the pilot replied. "Right when it happened—well, not right when—but in the seconds before—we lost all our Comms. They went out when we started losing altitude. We tried to call *MAYDAY-MAYDAY-MAYDAY!* but we couldn't reach anyone. I've been flying for a long time, and have never encountered this before."

Vince figured it probably wasn't the first time it ever happened. They were over Africa, after all. However, when he pulled out his satellite phone and tried to get a signal, he couldn't. That was a first for him as well.

Karl was outside the plane again, giving water bottles to both pilots.

"Hey Karl, you ever had one of these sat phones go out on you?" Vince asked, shaking his head in confusion.

"Just the one that got shot out of my hand. You know, the one right outside Jalalabad."

Vince hadn't been there, but he knew the story well. Karl had been calling in for close air support when an enemy sniper fortunately missed Karl's head, but unfortunately, put a bullet in the sat phone instead. *BAM.*

Vince was about to ask the pilot if he knew their location when a crackle of gunfire erupted from some distance away.

At least a klick, maybe two, Vince thought as he dove to the ground.

As he hit the dirt, he went to check the status of the lead pilot, also lying on the ground. Vince winced. Half the man's face was gone and blood poured from the wound onto the ground, inching its way toward Vince's position.

"Get down," Karl hissed at the copilot, who was crouched next to the cockpit.

The man looked back at the plane furtively and then toward where the gunfire sounded.

"Maybe if we surrender," the man puzzled, "maybe if we tell them who we are. It could just be all a mista—"

He never completed the word. A flurry of bullets hit his body in rapid succession, metal tearing through and obliterating the man's flesh. Vince knew the copilot was dead even before he hit the ground.

Vince shot Karl a *What should we do next?* look. Their options were restricted. The terrain was vast, wide open, providing them no cover. If they moved away from the plane they would be sitting ducks; but hell, they already were sitting ducks. He could feel an invisible force of evil moving closer. He saw the rounds tearing through the sky overhead. Due to the seemingly endless barrage, Vince estimated there were at least twenty men, maybe more, raining bullets on them. That was a lot of firepower, especially considering Karl and Vince had no weapons to protect themselves.

Then to his complete surprise, something both horrible and wonderful occurred. He hadn't noticed the sky turning black. It began as a couple of raindrops, but within mere seconds a torrential wave of rain poured from the heavens. He could barely see Karl, who was only ten feet away. Soon, Karl was able to locate him through the near-blinding rain and was yelling in his ear.

"We need to go. We need to go *now!*"

That's when Vince remembered that he had something that might help them, but not if he waited long. It had been a gift from a friend – a new but good friend. Vince had helped him in the recent past, and Vince harbored no doubt he would help them, if at all possible. He delved into his pocket and pulled out a pack of cigarettes.

Karl looked at him like he was nuts, but Vince ignored him. He tore through the packet. The already-sodden tobacco sticks fell to the ground and were washed away in the newly created, raging streams. Tucked inside the cigarette pack was something that resembled a credit card, but once Vince depressed his finger on the bottom right corner, a screen lit up. He'd been told he'd only get one shot at using this device. Once used, it would be useless. "One shot, one kill," his friend had said. It was securely encrypted. It would send a signal up to a private satellite, after which Vince's friend would receive its message.

He typed out the message quickly, pressed the send button and waited for the green light to know the transmission was successful. Although its burst battery power was now expended, Vince snapped the card in half and shoved it back in his pocket. There was no sense leaving behind evidence.

Now came the hard part. They needed to somehow find themselves a safe haven while trudging through the blinding rain, holding onto hope that the heavens would give them more than a few minutes of cover.

CHAPTER TWO

C al Stokes leaned back in his rust-encrusted metal chair and stifled a yawn with the back of his hand. The room he was sitting in stunk like elephant dung incense sticks and he winced as the taste assaulted his tongue.

"Don't tell me you're getting tired of this already, Cal," boomed Master Sergeant (MSgt) Willy Trent's baritone voice from the corner. There was no need for them to be quiet. They were two levels underground and plenty of concrete stood between them and any prying ears. "Here," Trent said, as he tossed Cal something.

Cal snatched it out of the air and examined the small package. "Gum?" Cal asked. Trent shrugged as if it was the only logical solution to the noxious problem. Cal sighed in resignation, popping one of the pieces of bubble gum out of its wrapper. Maybe it would help the smell. He placed it in his mouth and started chewing. *Nope, still smells.*

He couldn't wait to get out of this place. Their hosts had been proud to exclaim that they had been given a piece of prime real estate—a place to accomplish good work. If this was prime real estate, Cal Stokes was a flying monkey with gossamer wings.

"Man, remember the old days when we pumped in mariachi music, kept people awake, slapped them around a little bit, and just made their lives miserable until they told us the truth?" Gaucho asked from his location. There he'd laid out a bedroll and stretched his burly form to its just over five-foot potential. "Now you've got Doc in there with his potions and we don't get to have any fun. I don't understand why we all had to come out for this one anyway."

The Hispanic former Delta operator was just ruminating aloud. Cal would never interpret a comment from any of these men as an accusation or direct threat to his authority. Together they'd been through too much and they all bitched and moaned. Well, except for Daniel. The Marine sniper had his chair leaning against the far corner of the room, his eyes closed, but Cal knew he was hearing everything. Daniel Briggs was just one of those guys who was so in tune with the world that his radar never stopped scanning.

"What do you think, boss?" Gaucho asked. "You think Doc could use my help? Maybe I could put on a blindfold or maybe mess up the guy's hair or something."

MSgt Trent chuckled. "Yeah, you're one big, tough Delta operator, aren't you, Gaucho? Maybe I'll put in your retired military record that you like to tousle people's hair and give them wet willies. What do you think about that?"

Gaucho shook his head, but he was smiling. "I don't know, Top. Sounds a lot tougher than all that stuff in your service record about making crème brûlée or quiche or whatever you did in the Corps."

"You've told me you liked my quiche, Gaucho."

"I told you that just to keep you quiet. I much prefer your enchiladas."

Neither man could keep their composure now and they

burst into fits of laughter. Cal did too until the enhanced smell of the room invaded his senses again and he pinched his nose.

"He's coming," Daniel Briggs foretold, his eyes opening and his feet once more on the floor.

Cal hadn't heard a thing except the laughter of Trent and Gaucho. He was about to ask Daniel if he was sure until he heard the creaky door open as Dr. Alvin Higgins stepped inside.

"I believe you owe me seventy-five dollars, Gaucho," Higgins stated in his not quite Northeast yet not quite British accent.

Gaucho sprang from the floor. "What? Has it already been fifty minutes?"

Dr. Higgins shook his head, "Forty-seven minutes and thirty-three seconds, to be precise, my friend."

Gaucho grumbled but produced the bills from his pocket and handed them over to a grinning Dr. Higgins.

"I told you not to bet him," Trent said, his grumbled laughter slow and steady.

Dr. Higgins held up his hand, the one with the fistful of bills and said, "Now gentlemen, no need to argue. Would you, or would you not, like to know what our friend in the other room had to say?"

———

Two hours later they were lifting off the roof of the same building. The pilot was a salt-and-pepper bearded member of the Egyptian General Intelligence Directorate (GID). Altogether, it had been a pretty easy pay day. The request for their assistance had come from the CIA, Dr. Higgins's former employer.

An Egyptian businessman had been robbed of roughly

100 million dollars and the members of the GID thought it was tied to a young terrorist group working out of Cairo. The Egyptians wanted the best to determine the group responsible. Thus, the CIA had called on Dr. Higgins, who now worked for Cal Stokes and the Charlottesville, Virginia-based The Jefferson Group (TJG). TJG performed consulting work, most of which revolved around security and international relations. However, there was the occasional request for Higgins's interrogation savvy.

Dr. Higgins always wore a tweed jacket with a red handkerchief, even during this sojourn in Egypt. He knew how to pry truth from the most stubborn of men and was behind much of the interrogation reform at the Central Intelligence Agency. From the day he was hired by the CIA, he'd advocated for more humane tactics during the interrogation of prisoners. In fact, Dr. Higgins had perfected techniques to the point he barely had to lay a finger on any of his subjects.

His secret lay in the concoctions he'd perfected over the years. Somehow, during the 90s, he'd convinced the CIA to send him back to university to become a medical doctor, get his Pharmacology degree and a specialty in Anesthesiology. He'd singlehandedly pioneered a new realm by melding the use of mind-altering drugs with psychology. This ensured subjects were safe and more than willing to comply with his directions and answer his questions. It truly was a glorious combination.

The Egyptian official who had taken custody of the man who'd been interrogated was quite pleased with the information Higgins had extracted. They'd suspected that the man tied to the gurney was some mid-level moneyman for the terrorist organization. They'd hoped to get a few crumbs, but Higgins had exceeded their expectations. Within an hour and with a willing smile, the man had been only too happy to provide the names of the men in charge of the financial arm of the responsible organization.

Cal was still amazed at Higgins's work. He never asked for credit and was always looking to perfect his techniques. There wasn't a man at The Jefferson Group who didn't respect Higgins and all he did. He might look like Santa Claus's cousin with his portly belly, but all TJG operators treated him as an equal team member when he accompanied them on missions.

Cal tried not to think about what the Egyptians would do to the man in the basement. Now that the information had been extracted, he'd either be put in a solitary cell for the duration of his life, possibly beaten and tortured, or he could just be killed. Cal had to remind himself that wasn't his problem. To the former U.S. Marine Staff Sergeant, a terrorist was the lowest of the low, willing to kill women and babies if it suited their purposes.

But now it was an Egyptian matter. Cal and his men had done their part to help. Since they were not in need of money, they were not motivated solely by money. They had taken this job to keep busy.

By the time they returned to the Presidential Suite at the Marriott overlooking congested Cairo, Cal had resolved to take the first flight home. He missed Charlottesville, and he missed his girlfriend, Diane Mayer. She was currently doing a stint in Dam Neck with the Navy, receiving follow-on training as a Naval Intelligence Officer.

Cal was just about to repack his bag when Daniel walked into the suite they shared. When they were on the road, Cal and Daniel always bunked together. Well, unless Diane was along for the ride.

"I just got a call from Neil," Daniel stated, referring to The Jefferson Group's head of the Technology and Development division. "He says he needs you and Gaucho on the phone NOW."

"Did he say what it was about?" Cal asked.

Daniel shook his head.

When they arrived in the adjoining suite, the mismatched pair of Gaucho and huge MSgt Trent were digging through heaping plates of room service food. They looked up when Cal and Daniel entered the room.

"What's up?" Gaucho asked, his mouth full to bursting.

Daniel held up their secure phone. "Neil wants to talk; he's got some news."

Gaucho and Trent both cocked their heads. The repartee between this duo reminded Cal of the movie *Twins* with Arnold Schwarzenegger and Danny DeVito. The characters were so different and yet their mannerisms somehow matched at strange moments like this, just like Gaucho and Trent.

Daniel dialed Neil's number and placed the phone on the table. A moment later Neil's voice came over the receiver, loud and clear. "Cal, you there?" Neil asked.

"Yeah, I'm here," Cal said, "And I've got Daniel, Gaucho, and Top with me. What's going on?"

There was a pause followed by the scratching sound as the encryption took hold. Then Neil's voice returned.

"We had an emergency message come in. It's from your friend, Vince Sweeney."

"Did he use the E.T. phone home?" Gaucho blurted, a bit of bread falling out of his mouth.

Cal heard Neil exhale before saying with exasperation, "You know, I don't like it when you guys call it that." Neil Patel had originally named the small emergency one-time device something technical, but Cal couldn't remember the name. Like most of Neil's inventions, The Jefferson Group operators always renamed them for the purpose the devices served. Therefore, the tiny device had been christened "E.T. phone home." It made sense to them, if not to Neil.

"Yeah, he used it," Neil confirmed.

"What did he say?" Cal asked, glancing over at Gaucho, now on his feet.

It was Gaucho who'd introduced Cal and his team first to Karl Schneider and then Vince Sweeney. They'd helped The Jefferson Group when a bunch of idiots thought it was a good idea to try to get the Marine Corps disbanded. Sweeney's men had uncovered the leak or at least found the trail that led to the ringleader.

"I'm still triangulating the signal to determine their last location. I'm not sure why, but it's not as clear as it should be; I can figure that out later. I do know that it's somewhere along the Eastern coast of Africa."

"What did the message say?" Cal interrupted.

"Well, that's the other part that has me concerned. The message didn't come through in its entirety. It was a little clipped. I really don't understand how that happened. You know I tested it all over the world. The variables were all aligned and the satellite placement was perfect. I just don't understand how—"

"Neil, what did the message say?" Cal asked again, his frustration apparent.

"What? Yeah, sorry," Neil said, refocusing. "Here, I'll read it verbatim. *Plane down, possibly shot.* Then there's a blank, *forces firing*, another blank, and then the word *dead* and a period. *Will E and E. Ask your best friend in Washington about the details.* That's it."

Most of the message made it clear as to what occurred, but there were holes. Some kind of plane Sweeney was on had been shot down. Maybe they'd been attacked on the ground. E & E meant that he was going to escape and evade - basically hide and try to get away from the enemy. Cal's best friend in

Washington—well, there was only one person that fit that description because he didn't have many friends in Washington.

Cal said, "Thanks, Neil," and terminated the call. If Vince Sweeney had popped a flare and called for help, he was in *deep* trouble. Time was of utmost importance; therefore, Cal didn't hesitate to dial the number from memory. There was a series of clicks and whispers of vague sounds before the president of the United States answered the phone.

CHAPTER THREE

The crowds cheered and waved as Congressman Antonio "Tony" McKnight waved back, flashing a wide smile. He'd graced the covers of *Forbes*, *GQ*, and just the day before was approached by *Men's Health*. He wouldn't pose shirtless, of course, but the writers had claimed America wanted to know more about him and, of course, his health secrets.

A group of girls in the front row begged for autographs but McKnight pretended not to hear their pleas. He observed the crowd and frowned inwardly when he saw how close they had been to the barriers. He knew what that meant.

He gave one final wave and yelled out "God Bless America" before exiting the stage. His lead handler was at his side ready to spew out the pertinent details of their next campaign stop.

"How many people were present?" McKnight snapped.

"Five thousand," the woman declared without looking up, her eyes glued to her tablet.

McKnight stopped and his head swiveled slowly. She

turned to face him, her glasses perched on the end of her delicate nose.

"That did not look like five thousand – more like four thousand, Sonya."

She looked uncomfortable for a moment. "I promise, Congressman, we'll have more at the next stop." Congressman McKnight gave her a curt nod and walked away, leaving her in his wake. He didn't need the details of the next stop. It was just another Californian town - one of the endless stops in a primary campaign for the presidential election. He was well behind the leader, and he needed California if he were to have any chance to clinch the nomination.

He was almost to the door of the tour bus with *McKnight for President* splashed across the side, his perfectly tanned face welcoming the public to vote for him. He groaned at the thought of boarding the bus again. Running for Congress had been one thing, but running for the presidency was a marathon with no ending in sight. Scratch that, there was an ending, and if he wasn't careful, it would come much sooner than he'd expected.

The Republican congressman from Miami, Florida had entered the race as *the* frontrunner, but a few missteps and missed opportunities had nearly crippled his campaign. They'd clawed their way back to second place, but the former governor of Texas, a shrewd woman who had served twenty years in the Army as an attorney, was making a valiant play. She'd outflanked him on foreign policy, immigration, and even matters concerning the economy. As a senior member of the Armed Services Committee, Congressman McKnight had, at one time, almost seen the writing on the wall, but it wasn't in his blood to give up. He had never given up.

He was about to step back onto the bus when somebody called out his name. It wasn't a well-wisher or a potential voter but instead a man he hadn't seen in months. When McKnight looked at the man, one word came to his mind – lumpy. While McKnight prided himself on his appearance, this man seemed to take great pleasure in looking slovenly and unkempt.

McKnight reluctantly gestured the man over, informing his security detail to provide them privacy. They spread out to make a wider cordon to give the congressman his space.

"That was a fine speech," the man declared. "I always wondered whether you guys change it up for every stop or if you just switch Bakersfield for San Diego in your notes."

McKnight frowned. The man was teasing him. Chiding was this man's special gift in order to get under the congressman's skin.

"It's been months," McKnight said. "Please tell me you've come to provide an update rather than give me your tips on what I should or should not say at the next campaign stop."

McKnight crossed his arms over his chest and waited. The man known only to him as "Jim," though he suspected it wasn't the man's true name, grinned and flashed cigarette-stained teeth. McKnight groaned to himself as he spotted a remnant of the man's lunch wedged between two corn-colored choppers.

"It looks like your ship just came in, Congressman," Jim said.

McKnight's heart leapt. This was what he'd been waiting for and the only reason he'd taken a chance with the slob standing in front of him.

"Tell me," McKnight said.

"Your intel was spot on. They shot them down before they could get a message out."

McKnight wanted to pump his fist in the air and scream in victory. It had been a delicate situation. He'd heard about the covert operation from none other than the president himself. If all went his way, he would be soon run against the president in the general election. The irony of the entire situation was President Brandon Zimmer considered Congressman Tony McKnight both an ally and confidante. Thus, he'd seen nothing wrong with confiding in McKnight about his concerns as well as what he meant to do to alleviate the problem.

It had all come at a perfect moment for McKnight, who was floundering from the latest attack leveled by his opponent. Sure, it could be construed as treason, but what the president had done wasn't exactly legal either: sending special warfare operators in disguise to spy on a supposed ally. Well, how aboveboard was that?

At least that's how McKnight saw it. It hadn't taken much nudging in his mind to determine whether or not he would use the information for his own benefit. This was politics after all, and politics was war. Just like the generals of old, men like Julius Caesar, Napoleon, and even Dwight D. Eisenhower, rose from the ranks to become leaders of their country. McKnight, a man with lofty goals, believed he was doing the same.

The political world had been a perfect match for him from the first day they shook hands. He'd been seeking something his entire life, and when someone had suggested he run for public office, he jumped at the opportunity. It had really been a bet, and in those days, Tony McKnight always took a bet he knew he could win. He'd won that first contest and, from that first run, every win made his political aspirations rise.

Now he was vying for the ultimate prize, securing the White House. The path was still cluttered with obstacles, tripwires and moats. He'd have to use every trick he'd ever learned and call on all the contacts he could squeeze to pull out this victory. So he had made a deal. Sure, elections were about debates and how photogenic you appeared, but you could have those things in addition to a great message and a solid platform to build a presidency on. The dirty truth was you needed endless money to truly win. That's what always made McKnight laugh.

Everyday citizens polled were vehement in stating that they had voted for a guy because they believed in his immigration policy, because gun control was something they did or did not hold dear, or because they'd always voted Democrat or Republican since the days of FDR. What always surprised McKnight was how easily such people could be manipulated. All it took to sway their votes was leaking a negative story to a news outlet or having an inappropriate picture posted on a website that had the ability to spread like wildfire. Thus once ardent fans became lifelong haters – this was helpful in stealing votes from opponents.

McKnight had never been so naïve, because he saw democracy for what it truly was – a mechanism to manipulate and control the populace by the politicians that demanded reelection. Money was the key because without endless amounts, you couldn't win. Sure, you could pick up a councilman's chair or a seat on your local school board, but if you wanted to run, really run, you had to have not millions but billions behind you. This requirement, he lacked. There had been promises, but once the tide had swayed against him, the influx of money into his coffers had shriveled up.

That's where Jim came in. Jim was one of those guys that nobody liked to admit was in your pocket, but they had always existed, and everybody knew it. In the early days, they'd show up with a suitcase full of cash for some bigwig running for office in New York. Someone who somehow had the ability to control the boroughs and the warring ethnicities. The game was still the same, although it had gotten a little more complicated and much more high tech.

The game comprised of promising one thing to get another. The deal McKnight had made had been a test, an act of good faith, so that his potential patrons could determine if he was worth working with, that he was a man of his word but of utmost importance they gauged if he would do anything it took to win.

McKnight had supplied Jim with the information, location, and had even found out what type of aircraft the secret operators would be flying. He had insisted that the operators not be harmed. He hadn't explained why, but in his foreseeing way he knew there was an opportunity there. Sure, they'd probably be tortured and interrogated, but a couple guys from Delta Force were tough enough to handle themselves.

"Tell me what happened," McKnight said.

Jim looked around once more making sure no one was in earshot. Then he grinned again. "It was just like you thought. They got eyes on, tracked the plane and jammed their communications. They got smart and used an explosive on the side of the plane instead of trying to shoot them down. You know those savages; they probably couldn't shoot the Goodyear blimp out of the air."

McKnight waved the racist comment away. "Just get to the point, will you?"

Jim had a way of stretching out their brief meetings, like the more words he imparted the more McKnight was going to pay him, even though a long time ago they'd agreed to the total sum.

Jim scratched his stubbly chin. "They reported seeing one body thrown from the plane before it came down. They think it might have been the stewardess."

"And the soldiers, what happened to them?"

Jim ignored the question. "Once they were on the ground, militia forces engaged the target."

"Tell me they didn't shoot them."

Jim shrugged slowly. He was in no rush to get to the punchline. If they hadn't been in public, McKnight might have grabbed the man by the front of his shirt and shaken him. Maybe a couple slaps would do him some good.

Then Jim said, "Both pilots were killed."

"And the soldiers?" McKnight asked again.

Now, Jim frowned. "Well, that's the damnedest thing. Wouldn't you know, as soon as the troops went in to get them, a downpour started. They actually explained it was some kind of monsoon, that they couldn't see anything, and by the time it cleared the two guys were gone. They're looking for them as we speak."

McKnight felt his chest tighten. He'd expected good news, had seen it in Jim's eyes, but he'd been fooled. The relationship had been contingent on the operators being captured.

"Where does that put us with our friends in Beijing?" McKnight asked, then realized he had asked the question a little too quickly. He didn't want Jim knowing that he was worried. He added, "Not that they can renege on our deal now."

Jim gave a slow shrug, as if the details didn't matter. "They're pissed off, of course, but they're blaming the men on the ground for not finding them. You're off the hook for that part, but they did insinuate that the full amount wouldn't be delivered until a package arrived on their doorstep."

"What do they want me to do," McKnight grilled, "fly to Africa to find them myself?"

"That's way above my pay grade, Congressman," Jim said. "I suggest we sit tight and let the militia goons find them." He gestured his head over to the bus. "Shouldn't you be on your way now? Your schedule shows your next stop is in thirty-seven minutes."

McKnight was about to ask the man how he knew that

specific detail, but then he saw that Jim's eyes were twinkling. He was yanking his chain again. Despite his discomfort, McKnight grinned, held out his hand, and said loudly for anyone nearby to hear, "Thank you again for coming, sir. I look forward to your vote in November."

CHAPTER FOUR

Vince Sweeney recalled hearing once that water was the great equalizer. In his professional opinion, he'd always thought it was snow and ice. There were plenty of tough guys that, once they got plopped down on the top of a snowy mountain, would cry for their mamas and quit.

He'd never minded the cold much, but then again, he'd always packed the appropriate gear to keep him warm, and his athletic lungs hadn't ever had much difficulty acclimating to the high altitude. But now he had a new understanding of the toughness of those crazy SEALs and the training they endured—spending days in the water, ringing that bloody bell in Coronado. Cold and wet was his new hell. It wasn't that he was about to quit. He was far from that point, but the last thing he'd expected in Africa was to be cold and wet. It probably had something to do with the exhaustion and dehydration. His body was more susceptible to slight temperature changes; it was imperative to find shelter and rest soon.

"Did you happen to pocket an extra bottle of whiskey before we disembarked the plane?" Karl asked. His voice was low in the darkness, and Vince could barely see his friend next to him so deep was the smoky night.

"No," Vince said, "But I've got a couple Cubans, if you want one."

Karl chuckled and Vince thought he detected a shiver in the man's laugh; so he was feeling it too. Though neither he nor Vince would complain, *but good God, was it cold.* They'd both stripped down to their boxer briefs, tying their pants and shirts around their necks. They might not need them now, but once they got back to civilization, they'd need to look a little more presentable.

Luckily, they hadn't seen a soul for hours. They'd headed for the salt-engorged lake, thinking they'd skirt the edge and make their way as far as possible from the downed plane. Vince felt bad about leaving the two dead pilots, but there was nothing they could do about that now.

Karl froze, his hand in the air, head pointed forward. Vince stopped to listen, his eyes trying to peer through the dense fog. It wasn't raining anymore. The only sounds they heard, other than their own voices, had been the sloshing of their boots through the mud and wet underbrush.

"Did you hear that?" Karl asked.

Vince shook his head. "No. What was it?"

"I'm not sure. Maybe a—. Wait, hold on."

Vince sensed more than saw Karl crouch down. Vince matched his movement and then he saw it. Up ahead, there was a faint flickering of light. Not flashlights or anything electric. It looked warm, like the color of the inside of an orange; it was probably a fire. It reminded him of those old stories of southern plantation owners gathering for a manhunt into the swamps, torches lit, weapons ready, as their slaves ran for freedom. It almost made Vince laugh. Now the tables were turned. He was in Africa and he was being hunted.

Even though unarmed, Vince and Karl were far from helpless. The sight of light up ahead sparked Vince's senses and made him forget about the cold. He motioned for Karl to go right and he would go left. Suddenly his every movement felt amplified ten times. The sound of the splashing hit his eardrums like fireworks. He did his best to keep the sloshing to a constant ripple, and he wondered if they were making the right decision to go toward the light instead of away from it. But Vince's instincts screamed—if they were going to get out of this mess, they needed help, and help might be sitting next to that burning light.

Maybe they'd get lucky and stumble across peasants out for a midnight stroll, but what they really needed was a telephone. Luckily it seemed like ninety percent of the Earth's population carried around a cell phone, so it wasn't crazy to think that they might be able to borrow or steal one. The light up ahead flickered and disappeared; it took Vince a moment to realize the fire wasn't gone, but as he moved around, a small hill came between him and his objective.

Good, he thought. There wasn't much cover and any he could find was a welcome stroke of luck. The terrain finally opened up and Vince saw the origin of the flickering light. It was a small hut; it appeared more as a collection of rags pulled over taut sticks than a real shelter. As the clouds shifted, and the moon cast down an eerie glow, he saw that the hut was perched on the water's edge. From where he stood, it didn't look like a permanent structure. It was not a home for a family but a shack up on stilts to protect nomads from the elements.

He glanced to the right for his twin shadow, but he didn't see Karl. Maybe he hadn't made his way around yet, or maybe he was already there. It would've been better if it was raining to make the approach and conceal their movements.

Vince was careful now, each step measured, and then he heard voices. No, not voices, he corrected himself as he stopped to listen. He heard one voice, repeating something over and over. So he kept going, and as he closed the gap, he realized it wasn't talking. It was some sort of chanting or maybe singing. He imagined an old sunbaked man sitting in the hut, preparing his nets or hunting spears, mindlessly singing some old family song, whiling away the hours until the weather allowed him to resume his humble trade once dawn approached.

Then the wind shifted and the smell of roasting meat made Vince's stomach rumble. And that was why, a moment later, he was caught off guard at the sound of a snap of a twig to his left, followed by a curse.

Vince froze. There was someone coming followed by a shout from the hut, like a greeting or a question in some foreign dialect. A head poked out of one of the rough windows. Whoever approached on his left called back, unaware of Vince's close proximity. A smaller light, he guessed a butane lighter, snapped on. It waved back and forth in the air, as if signaling to the man in the hut that he was no threat.

In that sweeping light, Vince had seen the boy's face. He was no older than thirteen, maybe fourteen. It wasn't the skinny physique that concerned the Delta commander, but instead the AK-47 held in the boy's free hand. The man in the hut barked something Vince didn't understand. The lighter went out, and the boy continued on his way. What Vince needed was that rifle; it would at least give him some leverage. He didn't have to hurt the boy, so he slithered in behind the unaware youth and readied to strike.

He had to be fast and precise, and in the darkness, that wouldn't be easy. As a modern operator, he'd been spoiled with the latest night vision technology or at least a barrel mounted flashlight. Tonight he'd have to do it the old-fashioned way, the way his father had done it in Vietnam.

He was only four feet from the boy when a commotion erupted from the shanty. There was a clanging of pans, a yelp of pain, and the boy sprinted forward. Vince's hand caught nothing but air as he reached for the boy, who was too quick for his lunge. The kid was smart enough not to say anything, but rushed in without regard for his own safety. Vince was close behind and thought that he might reach the boy before he climbed up the ladder. Then he recognized a voice from above.

"I'm not going to hurt you, okay? Just take it easy," Karl was saying, but that only made the boy climb faster.

Vince had no choice but to yell up to his friend, "Tango inbound. He's just a kid." More noises from above could be heard as Vince leaped up to the fourth rung of the ladder and managed to grab the boy's bare foot. But the size nine foot was slick with mud, and it slipped right out of his grasp. The boy kept going, dashing right into the hut, weapon leveled and ready to fire.

CHAPTER FIVE

Karl tensed as the boy with the AK-47 slipped inside the hut. The Delta operator had one forearm securely against the old man's throat while his other arm encircled the man's torso. The guy was all sinewy threads; strong, but not strong enough to shake off Karl.

The kid came into the hut sweeping his gun, like he'd done it before, or maybe it was just the way he'd seen it in the movies. His eyes swept from the old man to the enemy holding him. The old man said something sharply, and he replied. Karl thought it might have been French, but the only French he knew was from half a semester during his high school sophomore year. But then he had gotten kicked out for fighting with Fitz Manzurela, so it was understandable that he didn't comprehend anything during the rapid exchange. What he did understand was the muzzle pointed straight at his head.

The kid moved back into a corner, and a moment later Vince climbed into the room, hands over his head — the international sign that he meant no harm. The old man said something again, but this time the boy didn't respond. Karl could see that he was quite comfortable behind that gun. His finger wasn't resting on the trigger, but straight and off, like he was still considering whether or not to shoot.

Vince moved a step closer and that's when his finger shifted to the trigger. "We mean you no harm," Vince said slowly.

Karl stared at the boy, expecting a confused look, but instead he detected a slight cock of his head, like he was more intrigued than confused.

"Who are you?" the kid asked in nearly perfect American English.

Well, I'll be damned, Karl thought.

Maybe they'd gotten lucky. But the AK-47 was still pointed straight at Vince and the lad showed no sign of backing down. In fact, his eyes looked even more intense now, like the sound of English had lit a spark to a tangle of anger smoldering in his chest.

Karl took a chance and released his hold of the old man. Instead of running to the boy, the old man turned and nodded his appreciation, like Karl had just served him a cup of tea. More words were exchanged by the two dark-skinned companions. Then the kid asked, "Are you Americans?"

Vince nodded and waited. Experience proved that could either count for or against you. While some of the world loved Americans, there were just as many who would kill you just for being alive.

"Yes, we're Americans," Vince confirmed. He lowered his hands to his sides.

"You sure don't look like any Americans I've ever met," he countered.

It took Karl a moment to realize what the kid was talking about, and then he almost laughed when he realized what he and Vince actually looked like. They'd been running around in the muck wearing only their boxers and boots. The remainder of their clothes were tied around their necks. *Yeah, they were a sight all right.*

Karl smiled and the boy finally lowered his weapon.

"What are your names?" their captor asked.

"I'm Karl, and the ugly one over there is Vince."

He nodded and was smiling now like the whole thing was one big joke, although just a moment ago he'd been pointing a loaded weapon at two trespassers.

"My name is Christian," the boy disclosed, "And this is my grandfather. Am I correct in assuming that you're the two men that escaped the plane crash?"

The blunt question startled Karl. Vince looked at Karl who shrugged as if to counter, "*What have we got to lose?*"

"Where did you hear about the plane?" Vince asked.

"A little bird told me," Christian announced.

Karl could see that the boy was enjoying the spy saga. "Hey," Karl said, "You want to tell me how you learned to speak English so well?"

Christian glanced at his grandfather, who nodded. So the old man knew English, but maybe chose not to speak it. There were a lot of those in third world countries, the ones who would only speak in their native tongue but understood every single word you said. Stupid Americans thought they were dealing with stupid peasants. Karl knew from experience those peasants were far more cunning than they were given credit for.

"I've gone to school in the States since I was five," Christian explained. "When I'm there I live with a family in Arkansas and go to a private school just outside Little Rock."

"Ah, so you're a Razorback fan," Karl concluded. "I'm more of a Crimson Tide fan myself."

Christian shook his head in what looked like exasperation. "Maybe if LSU got their stuff together they could knock Nick Saban off his high horse," Christian said.

That made Karl laugh. "You ain't so bad, kid. I'm sorry we ran into you like this."

Christian shrugged like it didn't matter. "I spend my holidays here with my grandfather." Christian shouldered his weapon and took a seat on the ground. "So now that we're all friends, would you like to tell me how you happened to crash land in the middle of Djibouti?"

Vince and Karl exchanged a questioning look. Karl wondered if Vince was thinking the same thing. *Who would have thought a kid like Christian would be the one calling the shots?* He was dressed in shabby clothes, like a thousand nameless nomads Karl had seen over the years, but his eyes were somehow clear like he understood the world better than the rest of them because of what he'd seen and experienced. If this was how Christian chose to spend his spring breaks, Karl bet he could teach a million spoiled American teenagers a lesson or two in toughness.

The Americans sat down across from Christian as the grandfather produced a large, clear water bottle and passed it to the men. They drank in deep swallows, relishing their first sips of fresh water in hours. Karl coughed after one particularly long swig, and his chest felt like it was on fire. He covered his mouth to stifle the cough, but he couldn't stop coughing.

"You okay?" Vince queried.

"Yeah," Karl wheezed, "Just went down the wrong pipe. I'm fine."

Vince turned back to the boy, not giving the incident a second thought. Karl was glad for the distraction as he continued trying to push past the pain burning in his chest. It had been there since the crash landing. Well, to be truthful, it had been there before that, but worsened after the explosion.

He rubbed his chest slowly and tried not to cough while Vince and Christian resumed the conversation.

"You said a little birdie told you about Americans in a plane? Now that we're friends, would you mind telling me the identity of that birdie?"

Christian looked to his grandfather again, and there was the same nod. "They don't really have a name, you understand," Christian said, "At least, not one really worth repeating. They're just one of the latest crop of mercenary entrepreneurs that take money to bully or kidnap." The way he said it made Karl think that the kid wasn't really concerned about the men who'd shot them down, like a bunch of local hoodlums that enjoyed talking tough without the ability to back it up. Karl doubted that though, considering that the same inconsequential thugs had just shot them out of the sky.

"Look Christian, I don't think it's fair to get you and your grandfather mixed up in this. I'm sorry we barged in like we did. Maybe it's better if we just hit the road," Vince offered, already easing himself up from the ground.

The old man waved his hands in the air and barked something at his grandson. "He says you should stay," Christian said. "He says he wants to help you."

"I have to agree with my friend here," Karl said. "This puts you both in a lot of danger, and that's the last thing we want."

More hurried words from the old man followed by a translation from Christian, "My grandfather says that the Americans have done much to help his country and to help his family. He means me of course. Without the scholarship I got through your State Department, I wouldn't be getting the education that I am today, so he says we're brothers."

Karl could see that Vince was mulling it over. The CO didn't have any children, but he had a soft spot for the good ones. "If you have a phone, maybe we could just borrow it for a couple minutes," Vince implored.

Christian shook his head, "No phone out here— it's kind of—tradition, with my grandfather. He likes to rough it, as we say in America."

The old man nodded appreciatively, bumping a fist against his chest.

That was it, Karl knew, but there was still reluctance in Vince's voice when he said, "Okay, we'll take you up on your offer. Thank you, Christian; thank you, sir," he said nodding to the grandfather.

The old man stood up from his cross-legged position and stepped in front of Vince, bent down, grabbed the sides of his head with his hands, tilted forward so that the two men were touching foreheads. He said something that Karl didn't understand. Christian was quick to translate, "My grandfather says that he sees good in you—that you're a good man— brave, a good fighter, and he is happy to help you. He would even lay down his life for you." The boy said it grandly, like he was the translator for a king, all seriousness with no shame in their openness. The old man let go of Vince and left the hut.

"He's going to prepare the boat," Christian said. "We might not be able to leave tonight because of the storm and the darkness, of course, but probably in the morning if that's okay with you."

Vince nodded then asked, "Where are you taking us?"

"The capital, if you wish, or maybe Camp Lemonnier if that would be better."

Camp Lemonnier had been a former French Foreign Legion camp. After 9/11, it had been leased by Joint Task Force-Horn of Africa (JTF-HOA), and was led by Marines from Camp Lejeune, North Carolina. Now it was a navy-run base and a key asset in the region. It was a perfect lily pad for the constant drone operations around the Red Sea and the

Persian Gulf, in addition to providing a good staging area for Special Operations troops.

"Let me think about that," Vince said. Karl wondered what there was to think about until he realized the dilemma. They weren't supposed to be in Djibouti. So while it might have been nice to walk onto an American base, there would be a lot of questions. The president had specifically told them to stay under the radar. Thus, that had to be taken into consideration; they could discuss that while they got dry and maybe had some food.

Another question hit Karl as they were getting up from the floor. He was confused about the situation he and Vince found themselves in. All voodoo or shaman nonsense aside, why would Christian and his grandfather be so ready to assist them? Finally, he inquired, "Christian, how can you be so sure that those thugs won't come after you and your grandfather?"

Christian smiled and pointed to where his grandfather had just left and asked, "Oh, did I forgot to mention that the President of Djibouti is my grandfather's nephew?"

CHAPTER SIX

The hotel room door opened, and a small brown form bolted through the door. Cal heard the curse on the other side and smiled as his seven-month old German short-haired Pointer, Liberty, bounded into the room. She was all legs, trailing her leather leash like a streamer. She didn't wait for an invitation before making a straight beeline to him.

Rather than make a jump for his face, or jump on his lap, she immediately sat down right in front of him, eyes wide, with her tail thumping back and forth on the carpet.

"How about the next time you leave her with me, you teach me how to get her to do that?" Johnny Powers asked from the door, his brother Jim right behind him.

Cal ignored the comment, paused for a moment before saying, "Okay," and then he leaned down to hug his puppy. Her body was shaking furiously with excitement. She licked his face twice and looked up at him with expectations of a reward. "Sorry girl, no treats today."

She cocked her head in dismay, but she didn't whine. Then, after waiting another beat, just in case Cal changed his mind, she turned and sat adjacent to his right leg and faced the door, as if she was now prepared to protect her master.

Cal kept his hand on her back, stroking her soothingly. "Did she give you any trouble?"

Johnny shook his head, but there was a slight look of exasperation on his face. "No, not really, but man can that dog run! If you let her off her leash—" He made a sign with his hand like a jet taking off.

His brother, a former Marine C-130 pilot, chuckled. "I don't even think I've ever seen my brother run that fast before. I should have gotten it on video."

Of the two, Jim was the more conservative brother; he was quiet and reserved, while his brother was more gregarious. Maybe it was the Marine in him that kept him that way, while his brother was all Air Force, smooth and slick. They were a welcome addition to The Jefferson Group.

"Did we miss the show?" Johnny asked.

"No," Cal said, "They're patching him through in five. The other guys should be here by then."

Daniel "Snake Eyes" Briggs was the first to arrive, walking in with only his customary nod to the three other men. Dr. Higgins entered without looking up from the paperback novel he was reading. The last to arrive were Top and Gaucho.

"You're telling me that you can really make that much money off a food truck?" Trent was asking.

Gaucho drew a cross over his heart and then pointed in the sky. "I swear on my mommy's grave," Gaucho said, "You should see how much money my cousin's pulling in and most of it is cash!"

Trent shook his head and whistled. "Well, that sure is something to think about."

"You thinking about making a career move, Top?" Johnny Powers asked.

Trent grinned, "I don't know about you officer types, but us enlisted men are always planning for our retirement."

Gaucho nodded in agreement.

"Thirty seconds," Daniel announced, walking over to the TV and turning it on. When the screen flickered to life, he ensured the camera had them all in the picture.

Cal hadn't even shared his concerns with Daniel. Earlier when he had called the president, his friend had politely put him off, seemingly unconcerned—no not unconcerned—guarded. That wasn't like Brandon Zimmer. The transparent relationship Cal shared with him was based on keeping no secrets from one another. Of course Cal didn't expect to know everything he was doing, but if he asked Zimmer a question, he *expected* an honest answer.

Then there was the problem with Delta. Gaucho had made discreet inquiries to his former unit, and at every angle he approached, he'd been quietly rebuffed. However, that could have to do with the fact that Gaucho was technically no longer a member of the elite counter-terrorism force. Once you were out, you were out.

But Cal couldn't shake the nagging feeling that something else was going on. When an operation goes bad, everything gets compartmentalized. Doors get shut, windows slammed, and either you're barricaded in or out. He felt like his team had been left out.

In addition to the president's uncharacteristic aloof response to Cal's concerns, the first levels of tripwires in his brain were starting to make imaginative leaps. He hoped those concerns would disappear once they talked to President Zimmer.

The flat screen on the bureau flickered again. In the next moment, the president's face appeared, then the sound settled. The president was on Air Force One, and alone. He wasn't wearing a tie, and his sleeves were rolled up to his elbows.

"Cal. Gentlemen," he said formally. Cal detected a hint of disapproval from Zimmer, like he'd expected Cal to be the only one on the call, but instead he got the entire team. What the hell was going on? "I'm sorry I couldn't talk before, Cal. I had forgotten how election years wreak havoc on schedules."

The lame excuse fell with a thud on Cal's deaf ears. "Mr. President, I'd like to know what happened to Vince Sweeney."

There was a moment of hesitation, and then the president asked conversationally, "Since when am I *Mr. President* to you, Cal?"

"Since you started dodging my questions about two men who, for all we know, might be dead right now."

Zimmer's eyes hardened. There were a few beats of awkward silence. Then Zimmer exhaled like he was suddenly tired, and rubbed a hand over his face. "How did you hear about them?" Zimmer asked.

"Does it matter?" Cal said.

Zimmer shook his head no and disclosed, "Look, this was supposed to be a discreet operation. That's why I called him in for the op personally. You, of all people, should understand that. How would you feel if *you* got called out of the blue, asking me about some secret operation?"

"Oh, I don't know. Maybe about as uncomfortable as we feel, finding out that two of our friends disappeared and could be getting chopped to bits at this very second."

Another awkward pause while the two men glared at each other; then Trent spoke up, "Whoa, whoa, whoa. Why don't we all start from the beginning? Let's not forget we're on the same team here."

Still the glare continued between Zimmer and Cal. Daniel

stepped forward and addressed the president, "Here's what we know. Vince made a distress call. He said they might have gotten shot down and were on the run. Neil thought it came from somewhere in Africa, maybe Somalia or Ethiopia. He can't get a precise location."

The president nodded, "Cal, I'm sorry. I didn't mean to get into this with you, and you're right, they are our friends. We all deserve to know the truth."

"I'm sorry, too," Cal said, "Now can you tell us what's going on?"

There was no hesitation now, like Zimmer figured the dam had been breached anyway. "Okay, I guess I should start at the beginning. It's been a few months. I was down in North Carolina and the boys at Bragg wanted to give me a debrief on a recent operation. It doesn't really matter what that was about because it has no bearing on this story. At one point, I got a couple of minutes alone with Vince, and we started chatting about China. Turns out that Colonel Sweeney is quite the subject matter expert on US-China relations. When you get a second ask him what he thinks about the South China Sea. Anyway, I asked him about Africa and the billions that are flowing from Beijing into the dark continent. He had his concerns, of course, like we all do.

"It wasn't until I asked him about Djibouti and the Horn of Africa that his ears really perked up. Now I'm not sure how much you guys know about what China's been doing, but they are putting a lot of effort into this new Silk Road, hearkening back to the days when they did steady business with Europe, Africa, and the Middle East. They want to revive that. A big part of that plan means increased shipping port access in intercontinental travel. Well, Djibouti is a small country, but it's a big part of the silk road because of its strategic location. They've got direct access to the Red Sea, a straight shot to the Mediterranean, and all those lovely ports there and beyond. The country's doing more and more business with other nations wanting access to their ports. Recently China invested billions into a few megaprojects, refineries, ports, factories, and now we've got word that they want to establish a naval base. Their diplomats aren't copping to anything about the naval base, of course, but we know it's in the works. That's what started Vincent's wheels spinning. I asked him bluntly what he thought I should do about it. He said the first thing any good commander would do is to get eyes on to determine what's happening."

"That's where we left it that day. It got me thinking, and after more troubling reports from my military and economic advisors, I had Vince flown up to D.C. for another chat. Apparently, he'd been thinking about it too, because he already had a plan."

"Let me guess," Cal said, "He wanted to see it for himself and maybe take a friend along for the ride."

The president nodded, "They went in with a good cover as oil investors looking for strategic partners in the region. As far as I knew, they had all their bases covered. The last I heard, they were on their way home, but then there was nothing. No word. No call. Then you called asking me point blank about an operation."

"Is that it? That's the whole story?" Cal asked.

"That's it." They were all quiet, digesting the news.

Gaucho finally asked, "That doesn't explain Bragg, Mr. President. I couldn't get any word out of them. Some of those guys I've known for twenty-odd years."

Cal answered for him, "That's their job. OPSEC is king. Brandon told them to keep their lips tight, so they did."

Zimmer nodded.

"So what now?" Gaucho asked.

"We're working on that," the president said, "The best we

can hope for is that Vince and Karl can make it out on their own."

"No offense sir, but that sure as hell sounds like they're getting the raw end of the deal. Leaving them out there like that. I know they're big boys but — "

He held up a hand to cut off the rest of Gaucho's coming remarks. "I know. I'm not saying we're doing nothing, but you've got to understand the position I'm in; there's a lot at stake here. The president of Djibouti is in a tenuous situation as well, despite the influx of foreign investment. They've been very obliging up to this point, but if they found out that we're sending in soldiers to snoop on one of their biggest investors —that might not sit well."

Cal could see that Gaucho wanted to press. Hell, *he* wanted to press the president. No one would, though. That was one of the benefits of being a soldier. You rarely had to take politics into account. Since he'd met Brandon Zimmer, Cal had come to understand more fully how heavy the burden was when you truly had to take everyone's interests into account. Luckily that wasn't Cal's job.

He was about to ask if they'd considered using any of the troops at Camp Lemonnier, maybe under the pretense of a training operation out in the boonies, but at that moment the president's head turned. He put up a finger for them to wait. He nodded to whomever had come in before saying, "Guys, I'm going to put you on mute for a second. Hold on."

His head remained turned. Then Cal saw Zimmer's jaw tense. There was a curt nod, before he turned back to the screen. He unmuted the sound, his eyes hard now, and said, "Well it looks like the Chinese have made the decision for us. The Secretary of State just got an inquiry from the Chinese Ambassador asking why we have covert operatives conducting industrial espionage in Djibouti."

CHAPTER SEVEN

Those eyes—those damn eyes—bloodshot and yellow like someone had dripped red food coloring into a bulbous egg yolk. They burned into him—accusing and shaming him. He tried to wriggle away, tried to slap the unseen face, but he couldn't. He was just a kid again, his hands too small, ineffectual against the man's body. He felt his throat constrict, and then he smelled it, that awful smell. Like stale wine and onions. He winced and tried to turn away, but he couldn't. The eyes kept following him, and then just like that, they were gone.

It took Congressman McKnight a moment to realize where he was. Why did he have that dream? The smell and the eyes were so familiar. It had been his father—the damned drunk. If there had been an international prize given for worst father of the century, Tony McKnight was confident his dad would have topped the list of contenders.

But why the dream now? His father was dead. He had a clear conscience about what he'd done. He'd only been a kid, but the decision was easy and one he never second-guessed.

McKnight eased himself up from the hotel bed and

blinked a few times to clear the vision that had been stamped in his brain like he'd stared into the sun too long. Now the smell had moved to a taste and it made him want to spit on the floor. He shook the thoughts away and tried to clear his head.

Why that dream? Why now?

He washed his face in the bathroom, brushed his teeth not once, not twice, but three times. The smell and the ambient taste of his father had finally left.

Why now? McKnight thought. He was just slipping into a new T-shirt thinking that maybe a walk, or even a run, would do him some good when he heard a knock at the door. It was one of his always-present assistants. The only time he had to himself was in his hotel room, and even that wasn't sacred anymore. The staffer walked in without a greeting, already spouting off the morning's agenda. McKnight listened to him a moment, resisting the urge to bark at the boy, telling him to leave him alone.

"Hold on," McKnight said calmly, "That first meeting - the breakfast."

The staffer looked up, obviously peeved he had been interrupted. "Sir, the one with donor from Sedona?"

"Yes that one," McKnight confirmed, "Reschedule it, and I want you to tell my security detail I've decided to go for a run."

The look on the man's face was priceless. It was as if McKnight had just called his mother a no-good gold digger.

"But sir, there's so much on the—we just— "

McKnight did cut him off this time. "We've been going non-stop for weeks. I need a few minutes to myself. Make sure everyone else knows. Tell the security detail to be here in five minutes."

He turned to find his running shoes, cutting off any further rebuff from the staffer. The kid did his job. Less than a minute later McKnight's phone dinged. The morning schedule, already reworked. *Good. Maybe a few miles and some sweat will get that damn bastard out of my head.*

It worked. Less than an hour later he was back in his hotel room showering and refocused. He couldn't remember the last time he'd had a muddled day. It was no way to start off a morning. He was always looking forward, facing down the path instead of behind, but as he combed his hair he couldn't help but wonder what other surprises the day might hold.

The thirty-minute breakfast with the wine baron transformed into a five-minute ride to the next event. The donor didn't seem to mind. He was more concerned with getting a selfie with the congressman to send his daughter proof that his money had bought time with the future president. McKnight took it all in stride, knowing that if the Chinese didn't come through soon he'd need as many donors as he could get.

Just before lunch, after he had delivered a steaming pile of pizzas to one of his local campaign offices, a message came through. It was his moneyman. The first couple sentences did not put McKnight at ease. The Chinese were still dragging their feet. The American operatives had yet to be found. As a result, the deal was incomplete. That was the bad news, but as he scrolled through the moneyman's explanation, the next part came into stark focus—the good news.

The Chinese were offering him an olive branch, a token of goodwill to the future president of the United States. Those were the moneyman's exact words. A bit too melodramatic for McKnight, but hell, he needed some good news. He scrolled down further. A brief explanation and then a series of pictures and then, wide-eyed with sudden excitement, there was a video. *There was a goddamned video.* "Yes," McKnight muttered under his breath.

One of his staffers asked, "Did you say something, Congressman?"

McKnight shook his head, "No, I'm fine. Thank you, just some good news."

"Are we almost there?" the staffer asked the driver.

The driver looked back over his shoulder and announced, "Fifteen minutes, Congressman."

McKnight didn't even hear it.

Perfect. Just perfect. He replied to the moneyman's message and instructed him to disseminate the information in any way he saw fit, but to wait until McKnight had a chance to make his own public statement. He wanted to light the fire and then watch it rage. He tapped send. Off skittered the message, blazing through encrypted protocols in a twisted path much like McKnight's own.

Maybe that dream had just been an omen that his father was watching and obviously jealous. Yes, that had to be it. Well, McKnight would show his father. He would show that piece of crap despite everything he'd said and put young Antonio through, that young boy was now a man, and that man was reaching for the stars. Soon he would control the stars and then forever he would stamp out his father's memory.

CHAPTER EIGHT

Karl insisted he was fine, but Vince knew otherwise. At first he thought it was just fatigue, but he knew there was something really wrong as they made their way across the lake. Its choppy surface cast them this way and that, and if not for Christian's catlike quick reflexes, Karl would have gone overboard. Karl normally would have been concerned by the near miss. Instead, he shrugged it off and became gruff to the point of being abrasive.

But even in the dim light, Vince could see that his friend's eyes were unfocused; he looked half drunk. And when he coughed it sounded wet, like a career smoker. Vince had seen Karl smoke plenty of cigarettes over the years. Hell, they all had. It was a perfect cover, but he didn't remember the cough, so it had to be something new.

When Vince asked his friend again if he was okay, Karl pushed him away, and this time sat deeper in the oversized canoe. The steady drone of the outboard engine continued as the hull slapped against the waves, one after another in a steady rhythm. Maybe he had been hurt in the crash. It was

possible. Vince had seen it before. You got hurt, yet all the
adrenaline coursing through your body helped mask the pain
so you could ignore it. Then when the adrenaline left your
body, the injury became apparent. He didn't want to press
Karl. He trusted him too much, but if there really was something wrong he needed to know now.

The voyage had been relatively calm and safe up to that
point, but as they closed in on civilization, there was a much
higher risk of being seen, and all four of them needed to be at
their best to get through it. Vince was sitting right in front of
the grandfather piloting the craft.

The colonel leaned close so only the old man could hear
him inquire, "Could we head to shore soon? I think maybe we
should all get some rest."

The man nodded his understanding, and then Vince felt
the boat veer left ever so slightly. Karl must have sensed it
too, because even though he sat grumbling to himself, he
turned to Vince and asked, "Where are we going?"

Vince pointed to the shore and announced, "I figured we
might want to hunker down and get a little shuteye for
tomorrow." Karl seemed to mull it over, as if he was deciding
whether to agree or throw in a veto, but in the end he just
nodded. Off the boat he continued to be sullen and
withdrawn.

Once they were on shore, they carefully concealed the
boat. The four travelers shared a single MRE from Christian's
backpack. While Vince felt like he could have eaten four of
the damn things, Karl only took small nibbles of the orange
pound cake. It appeared it took every ounce of energy he had
remaining. This was usually the time when Karl Schneider
was cracking a joke or giving his boss a hard time, but he just
sat there, nibbling away, avoiding eye contact.

But still Vince had to trust his friend to tell him if he was
in real pain. Some guys just went into a sort of hibernation

mode to let their bodies heal on their own, and now that he thought about it, he'd never even seen Karl injured, so he didn't know the man's telltale signs. Some men showed it on their faces, others in the way they walked or talked, and still others shut down, although that didn't happen often in the elite confines of Delta.

Vince awoke to an overcast sky which barely allowed the sun to peek through. He rolled over in their hiding spot to see Karl's face. He was asleep, but that wasn't what concerned Vince. His chin was red, like he'd dipped it in a bowl of paint, and there was blood dripping from it.

Vince shook his friend awake and when Karl didn't snap back to reality like he usually did, he continued to shake Karl until his eyes opened. It was quite visible to Vince that Karl was struggling to regain his bearings.

Vince handed him a bottle of water. "How are you feeling, partner?"

Karl snagged the water and chugged half the bottle before he realized what he had done to their limited supply. He handed it back apologetically. "What time is it?"

"Quarter after ten," Vince answered, "How did you sleep?"

Karl pinched the bridge of his nose, "I've got the damnedest headache. I can't remember the last time I was this dehydrated."

"You've got something on your chin," Vince said.

"What?" he reached down to touch his chin, the blood sticky on his fingertips. Karl's eyes darted from his fingers, to Vince, and then back to his fingertips.

"How badly are you hurt?" Vince inquired.

Karl ignored the question, trying to wipe the blood off on his shirt sleeve. When he was done, he still looked like a kid who had tried to drink too much Kool-Aid, and it spilled over, leaving behind a red stain on his skin.

"Are we hanging around here until nightfall?" Karl asked.

"Don't be a stubborn ass," Vince demanded, "If you're hurt just tell me, okay?"

The two men locked eyes. Karl was the first to look away. "I'm fine, okay?"

"No you're not," Vince pressed. "Unless you tried to make out with a rock last night, something's wrong."

"I'm not hurt, okay. It's not that."

"Then what is it, dammit? You know how it works, Karl, there is no *I* in us. We work as a team. If you're hurt, you need to tell me."

"I'm not hurt, okay?"

Vince could tell by his friend's tone that he was telling the truth. Then he understood, and his heart sank. "How long have you known?" Vince coaxed.

He half expected Karl not to answer, but he did. "Seven, maybe eight months."

"And how long did they tell you you've got?"

"Seven, maybe eight months," Karl repeated.

"And there's no chance?" Karl shook his head. "So what was all that nonsense about getting that place, starting the training company?"

"It wasn't nonsense, okay? *Goddammit, Vince.* Hell, we've had some good adventures, haven't we? I thought we might have one more. I thought I might beat this thing."

"You can't beat this kind of thing by yourself," Vince said. "Have you tried to get help? Have they offered you any treatment options?"

"Of course they have, but it's all crap. The first doctor told me it was terminal. I got a second opinion and the doctor didn't say the same thing but I could see it in his eyes. He told me outright that I was dying, and a hundred million dollars couldn't save my ass. So there it is. You want to give me shit for that, you go ahead. But you can't blame me for having a dream—for thinking that maybe you and me could build something good—so that maybe we could enjoy something we deserved. So just leave me alone, okay? I'll get through this my own way."

They were both silent now. Vince was trying to digest the news that his very best friend was going to die. It was different when you knew death was a possibility like jumping from a plane or breaching a house packed with bad guys. You knew you had each other's backs, but this was different. Hell, most of their careers they had chosen to gamble with their lives in order to protect others. There was nothing Vince could do or say. He knew at the very core of his being, if he could assume Karl's fate, he would do so in a heartbeat. And he knew that Karl would do the same for him, but that was impossible.

So he said the only thing he could think of, "Tell me more about that place with the red roof. How good of a deal did you say we could get?"

Karl grinned and he was about to reply when they heard the deathly familiar sounds thudding in the distance followed by mortar rounds raining down all around them.

CHAPTER NINE

One after another the rounds came in. From habit, Vince began to count the time between shots. They were regular, which meant it wasn't some hillbilly troop of rebels just lobbing rounds their way. There was somebody skilled behind those guns, but what really worried him was their accuracy. From the first shot they'd been almost dead-on—well, if they'd been dead-on, they'd be dead. There had been no direct hit yet, but Vince felt that it was only a matter of time. They were getting pelted by jagged rocks, and one of those could just as easily take them out.

"We need to go find the kid and his granddad," Karl was saying. The sickness that had been stamped on his features mere moments before had been erased and the warrior had returned. It was as if some unforeseen cosmic force had tapped a finger on his head and said, "*You will be a fighter once again,*" and the familiar steely-eyed gaze Vince had seen so many times before was back.

He could feel his own heartbeat elevate. Nothing crazy; he'd been under fire before. He took the mortar attack as a given, not really worried about why it was happening. He was more concerned about how they would get themselves out of it.

"I'll go check on them," Vince said.

Christian and his grandfather were about twenty feet away in another depression. They couldn't all huddle in the same hole, so they'd decided to split up, but they were gone from the spot where Vince and Karl had left them. He'd half expected to find them in the bottom of a crater from a mortar, but the hole was intact.

He ran back to Karl.

"They're gone; I'm not sure where they went."

"Do you think they ratted us out?"

"What do you mean?" Vince asked.

"Do you think they gave us up to the bad guys?"

That thought hadn't even crossed Vince's mind, but anything was possible. The coincidence of rounds on target was too demanding to ignore. Maybe Christian had lied; maybe they'd decided that it was safer to give the Americans up than risk their lives. Now that Vince thought about it, the story *did* seem too perfect. But no, he had to believe that the two men hadn't lied to them. For all intents and purposes, Christian was an American. Vince hadn't smelled a whiff of that fanatical air that he had gotten from a lot of kids Christian's age—the ones that kissed their mothers goodbye only to blow themselves up in the middle of an Israeli bus.

"No," Vince said. "It couldn't have been them. Maybe it was something else. Maybe they had—"

Karl cut him off and pointed up in the sky and said, "Look."

Vince looked up. There it was, unmistakable and unbelievable, some type of helicopter drone hovering in the sky. It was providing whoever was manning it a perfect view of the area. Vince cursed himself for not taking the AK-47 from Christian, but then his mind turned down a darker path.

The kid had said that whoever was after them was some ragtag bunch of locals, but he'd never heard of any kind of rebels or militias using homemade drones on a regular basis. Besides, the level of competency it took to fly a drone in conjunction with pinpoint accuracy of mortar fire suggested someone outside the Third World was heading the attack. He immediately ruled out the Americans. There's no way they'd be helping to hunt down the two Delta operators.

It could be that the Somalis or maybe the Eritreans had sent over some crack team to hunt them down. Money and prestige had a way of incentivizing such incursions. But why?

There was only one answer that made sense, and that filled Vince with the first hint of dread since their plane had gone down. It had to be the Chinese. They had to be the ones helping whoever was behind those mortars. They had the technology and the expertise, and that made Vince realize that their mission wasn't over. It was no longer an escape and evasion anymore. They had to determine, for sure this time, whether the Chinese were involved. They'd seen all the signs and monitored the construction crews, but to provide proof the Chinese were behind some Djibouti paramilitary force, that was something else entirely.

"We have to go find those mortars," Vince said. "Do you think you can make it?"

Karl's set expression was all the answer he needed. Dying or not, Karl was still a warrior, and he would never say quit, ever. One problem: they weren't going anywhere with that drone sitting up watching their actions. What they needed was a bit of luck, like that rainstorm the first day. Vince wasn't alone in thinking that luck was that special ingredient you could never expect, but when it came along, it always shone just as brightly as prior preparation. While no freak rainstorm showed up, maybe the next best thing did.

Over the booms of the landing mortars, Vince suddenly

heard gunfire, but it wasn't the steady staccato of an auto-matic fire aimed their way. It was one shot after another—steady, precise, timed—and the next chance Vince had to look up to the sky for the drone, he could've sworn he saw a spark flare on its dark hull. It was a long shot with a rifle, but still doable. He and Karl probably could've taken it out with a shot or two depending on the thing's armament and move-ment. There was only one explanation for the gunshots. Vince knew they came from an AK-47; it had to be Christian.

Karl had obviously arrived at the same conclusion because he said, "Come on, let's go find the kid."

The steady fire helped them zero in as they bounded from crater to crater, rock to rock, trying to keep their path as erratic as possible while still running toward the sound of the gun.

"Come on kid," Vince said under his breath, hoping that Christian would take the drone down before the drone oper-ator figured out where the gunfire was coming from and shifted the camera from them to the boy and his grandfather.

The silent request was answered, and Vince saw the drone tilt, first in a plume of smoke, and then it veered hard. The operator was obviously trying to get it back to whatever base they had, but it was no use. Another crack of gunfire and the drone was coming down, useless to whoever was behind it. The mortar fire fell off behind them now that the enemy's eye in the sky was gone, and for the first time in minutes Vince could breathe a little bit easier.

He thought he had Christian's location to the mark. He was right; a couple more minutes of stealthily heading that way, they'd found him. He and his grandfather looked unharmed. A little dirty, but no worse for the wear. Christian wore a broad smile, his pearly white teeth a stark contrast to his dark skin.

"Did you see that shot?" he asked, but then his smile

faded. He was staring at Karl. "Are you okay? Did you get hit?" Christian asked.

Karl shook his head and coughed once into his hand. Vince saw him wipe it on the back of his trousers. "I'm fine kid. Good shooting there. You really saved our asses."

Christian smiled again and Vince couldn't help but think how strange it was to see a teenager beaming while mortar rounds were still firing in the distance. He could make an excellent shooter one day. Calm under pressure. Vince filed that thought away for another day. If they ever got out of this mess, he'd make sure that Christian and his grandfather were well taken care of for their valiance.

"We need to find those mortar tubes," Vince said. "How well do you guys know the area?"

Christian turned to his grandfather and asked a question in their native tongue. They had a brief conversation and then Christian turned back to Vince.

"My grandfather says there's a dry creek bed not far from here. It runs up to some high ground where he thinks perhaps they've set up the mortar tubes."

"Can they see us if we head in that direction?"

The grandfather shook his head and motioned at the sand low to the ground with his hand. Vince understood that if they stayed low, they could probably stay concealed.

"Alright, we'll lead the way. Do you mind if I borrow that?" Vince asked, pointing to the weapon in Christian's hands.

Christian gave it to him without a word and he then pulled three more full magazines out of his backpack, handing them over to Vince.

"I'd like that back when we're done, if that's okay," Christian said.

Karl chuckled. "Kid, when we get out of this thing I'll buy you a whole armory of these."

It took them at least thirty minutes to get as close to the enemy position as they dared. The whole time Vince kept glancing at the sky, half expecting a fleet of drones to come out searching for their lost companion. But no more little birds showed themselves, even though there was a possibility that some predator-like unmanned aircraft could be high in the air, of course that took special flight clearances. Vince didn't think even the Chinese could get away with that.

There was one five-minute stretch when all sound stopped, the mortar tubes taking a break from their pounding, but then they resumed. The four travelers debated stopping as the first rounds went downrange, but they didn't rain down on Vince and the others. The mortar fire was focused at where they'd been hiding earlier that morning, so while the enemy was focused on their old location, Vince was on point, creeping closer to the enemy.

Then he saw them.

The four mortar tubes were arranged in a neat line on the far side of a small hill. There were two battered Toyota pickup trucks behind them, and a gaggle of fifteen or so men lounging about. There was no conformity to their uniforms as far as he could see, but as he watched he saw precise movements by the mortar gunners, loading in unison and calling out shots. There were neat stacks of rounds behind them that an ammo carrier could keep bringing to each gun.

Vince watched it all for a minute, trying to pinpoint the flow of the operation. It really had the laidback feel of a day on the gun range, and if he hadn't been on the receiving end of those rounds and had just walked up on the scene, he might've assumed that's exactly what it was.

Vince Sweeney had no problem with killing these men. The odds of this being some random attack were high if not extreme, and while he liked their odds, especially considering the fact that there were no guards posted and most of the men behind the tubes had laid their weapons on the ground. Vince was still wary about leading his four-man band up against twenty or more if there were some he couldn't see.

In the end it wasn't Vince or even Karl who made the decision. It was Christian's grandfather, who hopped out of the creek bed and marched purposefully toward the enemy emplacement.

"What's he doing?" Karl hissed.

Christian looked as confused as Vince felt. They'd just lost their element of surprise. First one member of the enemy and then another followed by all of them raised their weapons. They began shouting at the unarmed man walking into their midst. The grandfather had his hands up and was saying something rapidly but calmly. There were confused looks exchanged by the men by the pickup trucks.

"What's he saying?" Karl asked Christian.

The boy shook his head, "I don't know, I can't hear. The mortars, they're still—" and just like that, the mortars stopped firing. Now they could hear voices, the grandfather's clear above the others.

"He's saying, 'You know who I am. You know who I am,'" Christian translated.

It was apparent the old man was not offering himself as a prisoner to the enemy. The words spoken came from a position of authority. He was demanding to be heard. By now half of the men had lowered their weapons. The grandfather was speaking loudly again.

"He's asking why they are firing on him and his friends. Why are they doing the work of the devil in their own land?" Christian continued translating.

Then there was a commotion toward the back of the group, and Vince saw three more men running toward the pickups. One man stood out among the enemy troops. While the remainder of the rebel force had dark skin that ranged from cedar to ebony in color, this last man, who was yelling, looked to be of Asian descent.

"Bingo," Vince said, raising his weapon.

Now the Asian man was standing right in front of Christian's grandfather, but Vince couldn't hear what he was saying. There was obvious discord now. Vince could see it in their body language. Over half the men were listening to the grandfather while maybe a quarter took a less-than-resolute stand with the Asian man. Vince could feel the tide turning.

Christian said, "He's asking them why they're calling this man, the stranger, their master when in fact it is his own nephew who would take care of them."

This last question elicited the most drastic response. Now there were men backing away, as if being in the mere presence of the Asian would damn them for life. There would be no better time. Thanks to the old man, they'd taken back the mantle of surprise. It wouldn't be easy, but as an operator who'd fired millions of rounds over his career, Vince knew his shots would be true. He'd already picked out his first targets - the men who still stood behind the leader. The Asian man he would keep alive because he would make the perfect bargaining chip no matter the situation.

Karl understood what was about to happen. Without a word, Vince motioned Christian to remain behind but to take cover. The boy looked upset, but he nodded his assent, and he hunkered down further. No sense getting the kid killed; he had his whole life in front of him.

Vince had just taken his first step out of the creek bed and had sighted in on his first target when a roar from behind made him turn. Not one, but two Russian-made Hinds blasted overhead low enough that the rotor blast sent plumes of dust and debris up all around them.

For a split second, he thought that maybe it had been just a coincidence, they were going to fly by, and he'd have to come up with some other way of getting the old man out. But then the attack helicopters turned and weren't pointing in the direction of the mortar tubes. They were pointing straight at Vince Sweeney and his companions.

In the face of all that armament and then the swiveled weapons of every man who had been in the camp, Vince had no choice but to raise his hands and cast the weapon aside to the ground.

CHAPTER TEN

C al couldn't wait to leave Cairo. It wasn't that the place didn't have its charm; the country itself was steeped in a millennium of history. However, all Cal could think about was Vince Sweeney and Karl Schneider.

His team needed to get close to the action which involved flying into Djibouti. The president hadn't liked that idea and insisted that they wait for more precise satellite imagery, but Cal and his men were through with waiting. First they'd fly into Djibouti City and drop off Gaucho and Top. Then he, Daniel, and Doc Higgins, with Liberty, of course, would hitch a ride over to Camp Lemonnier. Gaucho thought he might still have some friends on the ground in the capital city, and Cal figured he and Daniel could probably pull a couple strings with the Marines at the American Forward Operating Base.

To make matters worse, the Chinese, and now the Djibouti government, were putting a full court press on the American president. Complaints were being drafted for the U.N. Cal knew that could spell trouble, not just for his friend, but also for them as they sought entrance into the country. A ban placed on travel could prevent The Jefferson Group from getting into Djibouti which would make their operation tricky. It wasn't that they couldn't find a way around it, but a straight shot sure would be preferable.

Everyone, except for the Powers brothers, were now gathered in Cal's suite making their final preparations. They were just beginning to discuss worst-case scenarios and the contingencies. All of a sudden Liberty bolted up from where she had been lying at Cal's feet. She was holding her head low and growling, pointing straight at the hotel room door.

Three seconds later came a knock, soft and unobtrusive, like room service or the maid would give in an attempt not disturb the guests inside. Liberty growled louder and more menacingly. Every man was up on his feet, and even Dr. Higgins had his hand in his coat pocket where Cal knew he kept his sidearm.

"Who is it?" Cal called out.

"Turndown service," came a female voice from the door.

"No, thank you. We'll be leaving soon," Cal said. They were met with the sound of silence, except for Liberty's growling. Cal moved to the center of the room while the others peeled off to the walls on either side of the door.

Trent scooted to the back wall where he could look out the window. "All clear back here," he said.

The next sound wasn't a knock but a crash. Three burly men burst into the room, their eyes straight ahead, and immediately locked onto Cal who had his hands behind his back. He tried to appear as nonthreatening as possible. He even smiled when the three thugs came to a halt.

"How can I help you gentlemen?" Cal asked, smiling.

"Where is he?" inquired the man standing in front.

"He who?"

"You know who I talk about. Give him back," the man continued in his heavily accented English.

The morons who were supposed to have their leader's

back had been so intent on him that they hadn't looked to their sides, but now they did. Daniel and Gaucho had their weapons raised. There was a lot of shouting among the three men like they couldn't determine what to do. The man in the lead must have told the other two to shut up because they did. Still the leader seemed unconcerned about their predicament.

"Where is he?" he asked again.

Cal smiled. "Look buddy. I have no idea who you are or, who you are looking for, but I can tell you for sure that you've picked the wrong time and the wrong place to come busting in here."

Cal couldn't tell if the guy totally understood but he still seemed unconcerned.

"My friends kill them now." He gestured to Cal's friends. "Then we take you to talk." He said something in his native tongue to which his goons responded with an obedient bark which must have been a "yes" or "yes, sir."

Stupid, Cal thought even as the silenced rounds from Daniel and Gaucho's weapons expelled, mowing the two men down.

To the leader's credit he didn't turn around despite the fact that he'd gotten a good splash of blood across each cheek and most certainly covering the back of his head.

"Looks like it's just you and me now," Cal said. "You sure you don't want to talk about this?"

The man laughed, and it was the first time Cal realized that he had an earpiece tucked deep in his ear canal. Cal didn't think but instinctually whipped his weapon around, shooting the man twice in the forehead before the enemy could squeeze off a single round.

The body hadn't even hit the floor when Cal heard Trent say from behind him, "Get down! Incoming!"

Cal had just enough time to hit the deck, holding Liberty

beneath him, when the windows behind them exploded in a plume of fire, raining down upon them broken shards of glass and pieces of metal.

After the initial concussion, Liberty was up and turned toward the window. Cal rolled over onto his back and saw five men on rappelling ropes, swinging in through the newly created hole in the side of the building. The massive form of MSgt Trent yanked one man aside before smashing the butt of his pistol into the attacker's face, rendering him unconscious. Cal was sighted in on the second invader and shot him twice in the chest. However, like the Energizer Bunny, the thug just grunted and kept coming after Cal. After two more rounds hit him in the face, his forward progress halted.

Daniel, Cal thought. He spotted him shifting his own weapon to the next target. These guys weren't pros or they would have come in shooting. Maybe they'd been given explicit orders to take prisoners instead of killing everyone in the room. Cal and his men were under no such rules of engagement.

A third man was down. The man in the middle was suddenly covered with a face full of fur. Liberty was ripping and tearing, and for a moment, Cal watched his dog with wonder. The man was screaming, and his blood gushed from his face. When he tried to fling the puppy off his body, she hung on with twice the tenacity. As Liberty held the man down, Cal was able to put two rounds in the man's belly.

There was one man left now. Daniel and Gaucho were closing in on him with extreme caution. Cal wondered why they didn't just shoot him until he took a closer look. It was then he saw that under his assault rifle their attacker held something else - a grenade. It was the old-fashioned pineapple kind, and the pin was pulled out. The man didn't have to say anything; his intent was clear. If he was going down, they were all going down with him.

Everyone except for the dead or the wounded enemy were on their feet now. Cal was inching closer, hoping he could get the live grenade out of the man's hand. You couldn't just shoot him and hope that he'd hold onto the grenade and the spoon, giving Cal enough time to push the pin back in. No, the guy would die, drop the grenade, and take at least three of them with him to meet the Grim Reaper.

"You don't have to do this," Cal said. He even put his empty hand in the air. The man was glancing around him with furtiveness and buckets of sweat were pouring from his forehead. He had a scraggly black beard, and he looked like he could have been either eighteen or thirty-five.

"They kill me," the man said.

"Who will kill you?" Cal asked, trying to calm the man down.

"They kill me," the man repeated. He moved the grenade and held it to his chest. He looked like a child who was guarding his toy from the other kids on the playground.

"Give me the grenade," Cal said in a firm, yet quiet voice.

The man shook his head and Cal half expected him to drop the grenade. He was in a panic. He kept looking around the room as if willing his comrades to rise to save him from this tragedy, but then Cal saw the resignation flicker in the man's eyes. He swallowed and then two things happened simultaneously. Four silenced rounds came in from Cal's right shooting the man in the face and neck. His legs crumpled, and then a black shadow tore in. Cal, for a nanosecond, believed the form to be Liberty. Fear tore through his body as he realized Daniel had thrown himself onto the man. Of course it would be Daniel, his protector, always ready to sacrifice his life for Cal's life.

Cal was too late. There was nothing Cal could do except fall back and try not to get sprayed by the coming explosion. He counted down the seconds in his head. *Three—two—one.*

He was on the ground now, curled up in a fetal position. Yet, there was no explosion. He was surprised to hear first a chuckle off to one side which was joined by laughter from the hotel room door. Top and Gaucho.

Cal looked up to see them both smiling and he turned to where Daniel's mangled body should have been. But he wasn't dead. Daniel was leaning against the wall, tossing the grenade, without pin or spoon, up in the air repeatedly. He sauntered over and Cal watched the projectile go up and down. That's when he saw it, and Cal joined in the chorus of laughter.

Whoever had painted over the original coat of the grenade hadn't finished or it had gotten scraped off, but the light blue stripe going down the side of the Mark II's pineapple-like grids was now apparent.

"It was a practice round." Cal breathed. Daniel nodded, his smile grim. "Then why did you shoot him?" Cal asked.

Daniel shrugged and said, "I had to be sure."

––––––

After they'd had a couple minutes to take a breather from their near-death experience, Cal put in a call to his contact at the Egyptian Intelligence Service. The man assured Cal that he had nothing to do with the unfortunate incident. He apologized profusely while promising to escort some men over to fetch the two men who were badly wounded, yet still alive, and in addition they would clean up the rest of the mess.

When the intelligence operatives arrived it took all of thirty seconds for them to confirm the dead men were associates of the financier Cal and his men had been in Egypt to interrogate.

"How do you think they found us?" Daniel asked the scrawny intelligence colonel.

The man's jaw clenched and he kicked one of the dead

men in the side. "I think it's obvious that someone spoke, and I can promise you that the leak will be found and plugged."

Cal could tell by the man's tone that the fiery colonel would leave no stone unturned, but that still didn't mean that Cal had to let him off that easy. "Colonel, I was wondering if you could do us another favor."

The man nodded quickly. "Name it, and I will take care of it."

Cal had already been thinking that this stupid incursion by the terrorist thugs was a blessing in disguise. If what was about to happen actually did, and their travel plans were scrapped, Cal and his men would need another way in. "Colonel, is there any way you can get us into Djibouti without anyone knowing?"

The man thought for a moment and then nodded, his tone all business. "Yes, I have the perfect man for you. Come and let us talk on our way to the airport."

Cal took one last look around the room at its blasted windows, the hole in the side of the building and the blood-spattered floor. He motioned for Liberty to come to his side and wondered how much the hotel bill was going to be. And then he happily realized he wasn't the one who would have to pay for the damages.

CHAPTER ELEVEN

The lights above the camera intensified and the producer counted down. The whole affair was much more casual than his recent interviews. It had been orchestrated that way. Focus groups said they wanted to see the softer side of McKnight. They wanted to see him as a person rather than as a politician.

When presented with those concepts, the news network was more than happy to comply. The LIVE sign on the side of the stage flickered on.

"Welcome back," the female host said in a tone that was somewhere between cheery and serious. "This morning's guest is Congressman Antonio McKnight, who is a three-term Republican representative from the state of Florida and a current contender in the national presidential election. Welcome Congressman."

McKnight nodded. "Thank you, Joy. It's a pleasure to be here." The host glanced at some papers on her lap as if she really needed to and then asked, "Congressman, it's been an exciting two days for your campaign. You went into California a ten-point underdog and then managed to squeak out a two-point victory. How much of that do you attribute to the recently released information concerning your opponent's past?"

"I'd like to think that the people of California got it right, that they didn't need any prodding one way or another."

The hostess chuckled dutifully and then said, "But seriously though, Congressman, the recent allegations about the governor's past are troubling, don't you think?"

"If you mean the *alleged*, and I would emphasize the word *alleged*, accusation that the governor was linked to racially motivated hazing at West Point, well that's just outside my purview."

"But, Congressman," the hostess pressed, "exit polls clearly showed that this news swayed a significant number of voters in your favor. To make things even more interesting, now there are reports that the allegations actually originated from your campaign."

McKnight shook his head sadly. "I have not and will not comment on the governor's situation. She's led a distinguished career in the army and in public office, and I will not add to the smear campaign that is trying to take her down."

"But Congressman, this is a presidential election. To make matters worse for your opponent, no less than five witnesses are prepared to testify against her. What do you have to say about that?"

McKnight's face was stern now. "That's up to the courts to decide, not me.

"But Congressman—"

McKnight cut her off with a wave of his hand. "I've said from the beginning that I am prepared, and all my people know this, to wage a clean campaign. If these five witnesses want to accuse my opponent of something, that's their prerogative. Look, Joy, presidential elections can get pretty dirty. We've already seen that. I'm proud of my camp. We're staying above the fray and doing this the way our founding fathers would have wanted. We are a land of free people, and it's up to those people to decide who should be elected. Now I believe they're smart enough to look past lies and see the truth. In fact, I have to believe that or what is this all for?"

The hostess seemed momentarily mollified. Then she gave a little smile and asked, "Let's just say hypothetically, Congressman, that a candidate had a proven record of racist comments and actions. Would said candidate get elected today with our society being intolerant of racial division?"

"I see what you're doing there, Joy," McKnight wagged a finger at her, "and I'm not taking the bait. The governor is a good person and has conducted herself in an exemplary manner during this election cycle. However, on the topic of racism, you know my record. As a man of Hispanic descent, I've felt the crack of the racist whip. Our job as government officials, elected by the people and for the people, is to stamp out bigotry wherever it rears its ugly head. If I'm lucky enough to be elected president, I'll continue to do the same." McKnight's last words were the obvious end of his commenting on the topic and the hostess took the cue.

"Let's switch to another topic, Congressman. Foreign policy."

McKnight rubbed his hands together, and gestured to the hostess with a give-it-to-me gesture he was ready for the fast ball right down the middle. "Rumors are currently circulating about a Chinese complaint that could soon be sent to the U.N. Security Council. Do you have any knowledge of this, Congressman?"

"I do," McKnight said.

"And would you like to share with our audience what you know about the complaint?"

McKnight smiled. "Why don't you tell me what you know, Joy? Then ask me whatever question you'd like."

The hostess glanced down at her papers and stated, "Our sources confirm the Chinese plan to accuse the United States of industrial espionage and illegal covert operations in and around the Horn of Africa." When McKnight didn't say anything, the hostess continued. "Our sources go on to say that the Djibouti government is prepared to enforce a no-fly zone over their entire country and will soon ask the president to remand all U.S. troops to their current locations in the country of Djibouti. Congressman, were you aware of any covert operations happening in and around Chinese facilities within Djibouti?"

"Joy, I'm sure you and our viewers know that Djibouti is a very important strategic partner in that region. We've recently extended our lease to use Camp Lemonnier and expanded our support services in the region. As far as any specific operations, it's impossible to comment further due to national security protocol."

When it was obvious that McKnight wasn't going to address specific operations, the hostess swerved to the left.

"Would you say that this is an indication of the failed policy of the Zimmer administration with regard to the Chinese?"

"Joy, you really are trying to get under my skin today, aren't you?" But McKnight was smiling like he was enjoying the whole thing.

The hostess gave him a tight smile back. "Congressman, if you would please answer the question. I'm sure America would like to know your take on President Zimmer's diplomatic plans for the People's Republic of China."

"As I've said many times before, President Zimmer and I are very close. I'm proud to be considered a valued member of his inner circle. We've worked together through some very trying times, and I fully support everything he's done regarding China and Djibouti. I'll even go further by saying that some of those very ideas were my own, although I won't tell you which ones because—well—I don't really need credit for that, do I?"

The hostess couldn't help but give him a sarcastic look as if she was saying *Are you freaking kidding me?*

"But Congressman, this is an election year - a presidential election year. If things continue to go your way, you will more than likely be standing face-to-face with President Zimmer on election day in November."

"Well, Joy, I really hope you're right and if you've got a crystal ball back in that dressing room of yours, I sure would like to borrow it sometime. As for the election, I would be proud and honored to go toe-to-toe with my good friend, President Brandon Zimmer. I will tell you that it will be a fair and honest contest. I'm sure if you asked the president, he'd say the same thing."

The producer waved a hand above the camera, signaling that their time was almost up. The hostess looked across the table and said, "Thank you so much for stopping by, Congressman." She turned back to the camera. "Next, I'll be talking to a former State Department official who will give us the full rundown of what a no-fly zone over Djibouti could mean."

The LIVE sign went dark, and McKnight rose from his chair. The hostess rose too, and she moved in close, so close that McKnight could smell her perfume. Or was it her shampoo? She was pretty. She had the look of someone who was more bookish than outgoing. Maybe at one point she wanted to be a college professor, but she had been lucky enough to have the good looks to put her in front of the camera. Her star was on the rise and McKnight made a mental note to ask her out for a cup of coffee or maybe a cocktail, off the record of course.

"Congressman," the hostess said quietly so only he could

hear, "are you sure there isn't anything else you'd like to tell me about your opponent's current predicament, say that maybe your people were behind it?"

McKnight raised his right hand and smiled. "Joy, I swear from the bottom of my heart that those pictures, that video, and those witnesses did not originate within my campaign." He lowered his hand and stuck it out to shake hers. "Now, if it happens to benefit me down the road, like in our upcoming primaries, who am I to tell America that they shouldn't be fixated on that disgusting scene?"

The hostess' smile warmed like they were finally on the same page. She shook his hand. It was soft, but her grip was hard. "I look forward to our next chat, Congressman. Feel free to contact the station at any time. They'll patch you through to my private number."

McKnight nodded and then made the rounds, making sure to thank the cameramen, the lighting specialist, and the producer for their good work. Then his handlers were back, and he was whisked off to the waiting motorcade.

Once safely ensconced in the Chevy Suburban, he looked over at his greasy moneyman. "Please tell me that bitch is going to concede before the end of the week."

"My sources say it's going to be more like the end of today," the man said, not even cracking a smile as McKnight would have expected.

He was right. Just as *Primetime* launched across the nation that night, the governor of Texas announced that she would be suspending her presidential campaign in order to deal with the very serious accusations levied against her.

And just like that, Congressman Antonio McKnight was once again the overwhelming frontrunner with a straight shot to the White House.

CHAPTER TWELVE

Gaucho kept pinching his nose and rubbing it on the back of his hand as they exited the airport cargo terminal. "Man, I don't think I'll ever get that smell out of my nose," he said, rubbing his nose one last time on his arm before he gave up.

MSgt Trent chuckled. His friend was one of the toughest bastards he'd ever met, but man, did he have his dislikes. His first pet peeve was cold; not an issue right now. Djibouti City felt like it was on top of the frying pan. His second pet peeve was disgusting smells, which had been their own personal hell for the last three hours. The Egyptian intelligence colonel had been true to his word and arranged a flight to Djibouti for them. The only problem was the flight had been in the cramped confines of a sweltering cabin filled with dyed leather which smelled more like rotting animal flesh than whatever purses or wallets it was destined to become at some point.

"Come on now," Trent said. "It can't be nearly as bad as that sewer you told me about in Baghdad. How many nights did you say you spent in there?"

Gaucho made a face like he was going to vomit. "I told you not to bring that up again, Top. They were probably the two worst days of my life."

MSgt Trent shook his head and laughed again, slapping his friend on the back. "Then come on. Let's see if we can't find a couple beers to make that stink go away."

The mismatched pair took a meandering route through the city. The place was bustling as natives and foreigners intermingled around brand new cafes, hotels, and even a shiny new office building sprinkled here and there. Trent had been in the city only once before, but that had been before all the foreign investment hit the streets. Back then it had looked much like any other third world city trying to keep itself going. But now, outside investment had wriggled its long tentacles into the region, quickly making Djibouti and its open ports an important hub for the surrounding area.

Gaucho, on the other hand, seemed to be right at home. He was the one who flagged down taxi cabs and instructed the drivers exactly where to go. They'd go up and down a few streets, always checking to see that they didn't have a tail, and then hop in another cab and go off to another location. By the time they reached the rundown hotel, Trent was completely lost and told Gaucho so.

Gaucho just shrugged and said, "You tend to get to know a place when you have to scour a city to find a decent beer."

Trent had to duck under the sagging hotel awning to follow Gaucho into the hotel. They checked in under ficti-tious names and then paid the toothless man who was only too happy to take the cash out of the hands of the two foreigners.

The only people they encountered on the way up to their room were three nearly identical bespectacled men chatting away in German. They didn't even look up from their conver-sation as Trent and Gaucho passed.

They found their room easily. There was a tiny bed in the middle of the cramped room and a ratty couch set against the window. The window-mounted AC unit sputtered like it was trying to chug up a mountain. When Trent put his hand in front of the mold-covered vent, the only thing he was greeted with was more warm air.

"You want the bed or the couch?" Trent asked.

"Neither," Gaucho said.

"Neither? You planning on sleeping on this floor?" Trent shuffled from one foot to another. The carpet actually crunched under his step as if there were 30 years' worth of guests' crud soaked into the material.

Gaucho shook his head and walked over to the mini fridge. A waft of cool mist breathed into the stifling room air, and Gaucho pulled out two beer bottles, handing one to his friend. Trent popped off the top using the corner of the chipped and mangled metal headboard of the bed. He took one sip, nodded appreciatively, and then chugged half of the rest.

"Not bad, right?" Gaucho asked.

What Trent really wanted was a gallon of water, but a half a beer would have to do, so he pounded the rest before answering, "You want to tell me what the hell we're doing here? Because if we're not going to get any rest, maybe we should just hit the road."

Gaucho took his time savoring the beer and then gave one final throaty sigh of appreciation. Then he held up his own bottle top as if that would explain everything.

Trent looked at his top and said, "Okay? A lion and a giraffe. You want to tell me what that means?"

Gaucho tossed the bottle top to Trent who caught it and looked again at the beer maker's logo. "Turn it over," Gaucho said.

"Well I'll be damned," Trent said. On the other side of the

bottle cap was an address written in neat permanent marker.

"Can't say I've seen that trick before," Trent said.

"You're just a Marine," Gaucho said. "You can't expect to be an Army of One just yet." He was grinning and Trent threw him a disgusted look.

"What do you want me to do with this?" he asked, raising the bottle cap.

"Flush it down the toilet and take a leak if you need to. Then we'll go."

Five minutes later, they were headed down the back hall and took the rear exit into a back alley. Trent half expected to find overflowing dumpsters and poor beggars lining the thin strip of concrete, but the place was clean. Every scrap of trash seemed to be in its place.

"This way," Gaucho said.

After another thirty minutes of walking and two cab rides later, they arrived at their destination. From outside, the place looked like it was maybe five years younger than the hotel they'd left, but at least when they walked in the lobby, frigid air blasted down from oversized vent holes.

"Now that's more like it," Trent said, angling his face up to the stream of blissfully cool air.

"Come on, Top," Gaucho said without stopping. The Hispanic operator passed by a perfectly tailored man standing behind the welcome desk who barely registered their presence. There was a sign above a door at the other side of the lobby that said "BAR" in three different languages.

Trent noted the heavy sound of a roaring fan as they approached, and when he entered he realized there was a huge duct overhead that was sucking up the billows of smoke from the patrons below. Despite the empty hotel lobby, the bar was full to capacity.

The customers came in all shapes and sizes and only a handful looked up when Trent and Gaucho entered. They had to stand at the bar and have a drink before a table came available . They made small talk until a waiter appeared to take their order.

"Two more of these, please," Gaucho said, pointing to their beers. The man nodded and disappeared.

"So when's your buddy gonna show up?" Trent asked, staring down a pair of particularly swarthy-looking patrons. Gaucho shrugged, completely unconcerned. "You really live for keeping me in the dark, don't you?"

Gaucho grinned and shrugged again.

The waiter took his time coming back. Trent had watched him wander the room, depositing drinks, until finally they received the last two bottles on the well-worn tray. He set down two napkins upon which he placed the two beer bottles before walking away.

"Nurse that one, will you?" Gaucho said before Trent could pick up his new drink. The Marine gave him a quizzical look but Gaucho only answered by picking up his new beer bottle, laying his hand next to the wet-ringed napkin. Trent looked down, and just like before, what could've been in the same handwriting as the bottle cap, was the number 37. Gaucho crumpled up the napkin once he knew Trent had read it, then sat back to savor his beer.

They spent the next ten minutes each letting his gaze travel around the room as they chatted about nothing in particular. Finally, Gaucho polished off the rest of his drink, set it down on the table and reached into his pocket for a couple of bills. After laying them on the table, he stood and Trent followed. They made their way back to the lobby where the man at the desk once again ignored them.

They went up the stairs. The second floor had a sign that said, "Rooms 25-40 to the right." Trent pointed at it as Gaucho continued up the stairs to the third level. "Don't we want to go that way? Room 37, right?"

Gaucho shook his head. "Keep going, Hombre."

For some reason there were even more rooms on the third level and the numbering system didn't really make much sense to Trent, but he followed along, and soon they were at room 73. *Whoever Gaucho's contact was had switched the numbers.* Gaucho knocked twice. There was a moment before anyone answered.

The man who opened the door was about the squirreliest-looking dude that MSgt Trent had ever seen. He wore baggy clothes over his wiry form. He had the dark complexion of a native, but his hair was matted and caked with dust. His eyes darted every which way like he was looking for ghosts that weren't there.

He didn't say a word, but let the two men in and then closed the door behind them. As Trent stepped deeper into the room, he watched the man out of the corner of his eye. Even the dude's body was shaking like he had some kind of palsy. Gaucho was watching the man too, but he was smiling, like he knew something that Trent didn't.

And then, to Trent's complete surprise, the man's hunched form straightened, and where there had once stood a man maybe just over five feet, the guy before them now was probably closer to five foot six. More interestingly, his eyes were no longer twitching and his body was ramrod straight. He wore a sly grin matching Gaucho's.

"Top, I'd like you to meet Sergeant Elliott Peabody."

The man wearing baggy clothes walked over, stuck out a hand, and in an accent even deeper than Trent's own relatives said, "Pleased to meet you, Master Sergeant."

"Well I'll be damned," Trent said, shaking the man's hand that was surprisingly strong considering his size. Gaucho and Sergeant Peabody both laughed at Trent's discomfort.

"Sarge and I go back a long way, Top. He even carried me out of a firefight once. Where was that, Sarge? Panama?"

Peabody shook his head. "Poland, Gaucho. Are you getting that old? Startin' to forget things?"

Gaucho shrugged. "Maybe, my friend. So, did you find out anything?"

Sgt. Peabody motioned them over to the table. It was a little rickety but still serviceable, and they all sat down. "Everybody's pretty tight-lipped around here right now," Peabody said. "Ain't seen that in a while. You been watching the news?" Gaucho and Trent both nodded. "Well, word on the street is, there's a little power struggle going on inside the Djibouti government. Now, I'm not officially supposed to know this, but a friend of a friend of a friend told me that a certain Djibouti general ain't too happy with the president cozying up to us Americans."

"And who is this general?" Gaucho asked.

Peabody shrugged. "I don't know yet. That's what I'm trying to find out. My boss thinks there's going to be a coup, and that's about the last thing we need right now."

"Your boss?" Trent asked.

Peabody grinned. "I'm a card-carrying member of the Children's Institute of America."

The CIA, Trent thought. Who better to know what was happening on the ground than an operative from the Central Intelligence Agency?

"Has this general made any moves yet?" Trent asked.

"That same circuitous source mentioned they're going to start quietly rounding up foreigners. You know, because now there's suspicion considering what the Chinese have told the U.N., and said general is supposed to have the ear of the Djibouti president, even though the president doesn't know exactly what the general's going to be doing."

Gaucho grunted. "And you're sure there's been no word about any prisoners yet?"

Peabody shook his head. "Not that I've heard of. I mean,

there's the occasional kidnapping stuff, of course. That's to be expected in this part of the world, but for the most part, the government's kept that hidden, as you'd expect. No sense scaring off foreign investments, if you know what I mean."

Gaucho leaned further across the table. "Look, Sarge, I know I didn't tell you exactly what this was about before, but we're looking for two friends."

Peabody's eyes narrowed and he folded his arms across his chest. "Who are they?"

"Vince Sweeney and Karl Schneider," Gaucho said.

Peabody turned his head and spit on the floor. "Nobody told me about this."

"Nobody's supposed to know," Gaucho said.

Peabody shook his head. "I wish I'd known, because then I'd have been looking. Vince and Karl were good to me when us men of color weren't especially liked in the Army. I'd hate to see something happen to them. Tell me what you need me to do and consider it done."

"Just keep your eyes and ears open. Don't let your boss know what's going on, at least until I tell you. Also, we might need some of your assets soon."

Peabody nodded and put both of his hands on the table and looked at his watch. "I've been here too long. I need to go, but before I do, I want to tell you both to be careful. This may look like a cosmopolitan city now, but things are about to turn. I can feel it in my bones. So keep your heads down. If you're going to be in town for long, make sure you steer clear of the military. I don't like the sound of whoever this general is."

"Thanks for the warning," Trent said, and Peabody rose from the table and left without saying another word. When he was gone, Trent said, "Your friend is an interesting cat."

"Top, you have *no* idea." They waited another five minutes before leaving the way they'd come.

CHAPTER THIRTEEN

S o far the trip to Camp Lemonnier had been a total bust. Their plan had been to make contact with US forces without having to mention any of the strings they had back in D.C. Cal hadn't recognized a single Marine he'd seen walking by, and the only glances of a non-hostile origin they'd received were born of curiosity, staring at Liberty as she pranced along between Cal and Daniel.

They hadn't seen Dr. Higgins since they'd landed, but both Marines knew that the wily interrogator could take care of himself. Without any current options, and because all three of them wanted to get out of the heat, they headed to the chow hall. It was between meals, but like any military base, there was always someone manning the food stations for those coming off the watch or coming in after their patrols.

The only other people in the mess hall were a pair of airmen who looked like they might plant facedown into their trays of untouched food. Cal and Daniel both grabbed burgers, including an extra hamburger patty for Liberty and a handful of water bottles. They explained to the sergeant behind the counter that the German short-hair was a working dog, then they ate in silence, savoring their first American meal in over a week. When Liberty was done, she laid her head in Cal's lap and closed her eyes. It was her way of telling him it was time for all of them to take a nap.

"Half a day gone, and still nothing," Cal said. "You think Gaucho and Top found out anything?" Daniel shrugged and held out the last bite of hamburger for the dog. Liberty took it gently out of his hand, chewed it twice, gulped, and then she licked Daniel's hand in thanks. This time, she laid her head in Daniel's lap.

"Knowing those two, they'll find trouble long before we do," Daniel said.

"You sure about that? They say we are the trouble magnets, not them. Besides, I wouldn't mind a little trouble right now. You know me and waiting around. I don't have near the patience that you do."

Daniel nodded and polished off another water bottle. "When do you think we should bring Brandon into this?" Daniel asked, insinuating that they should use some of the president's clout to kick open some doors.

"We should wait. I know we're losing time, but it looks like El Presidente has his hands full. Maybe Doc Higgins will come up with something."

As if on cue, Dr. Alvin Higgins walked in a few moments later. He was sweating profusely, but he wasn't huffing and puffing from the heat, showing his conditioning in spite of his size. He pulled up a chair and sat down, while mopping his brow with a handkerchief.

"Gentlemen, I hope your investigations are going well."

"We've got zilch, Doc," Cal said.

Dr. Higgins looked from one man to another. "Why, I would have thought a duo of your stature and expertise would have been able find some kind of information by now or have at least dipped your toes into trouble. As for me, I now remember why I took an office job instead of jet-setting from one desert locale to the next." Cal could see he was building up to something. They waited patiently and Daniel smiled.

"Why, just as I was strolling down Camp Lemonnier Boulevard, enjoying the nonexistent breeze and dreaming of a nap in a nice air-conditioned hotel room, I happened to come across the most interesting fellows. It was near the front gate, you see, and this young boy was accompanied by an older gentleman, who I came to find out was his grandfather. Said young man was chatting amicably with one of the soldiers in fluent American English, even though he was dressed like a native. I casually listened in on their conversation and happened to hear two familiar names."

Dr. Higgins paused, wiped his brow before he continued. "Would you gentlemen like to venture who this young lad was speaking of?"

"Vince and Karl," Daniel answered. Dr. Higgins nodded.

"Naturally, I didn't want them to know that I was eaves-dropping, but I casually followed behind and watched where the soldier took them. I thought that perhaps the three of us —or rather four—excuse me, Liberty." He reached down and patted her head. "I thought the four of us could go find yon natives and have a little chat."

"Doc, you never cease to amaze me, you know that?" Cal said.

Dr. Higgins gave a short bow, and said, "I live only to entertain you, young Calvin."

Sometime later, they'd somehow convinced the layers of base protection, without invoking the president's name, that they weren't a threat and that they needed to talk to the commanding officer of the camp. He greeted them with curt civility and got straight to the point.

"I'm not sure who you folks are, but my adjutant says that

you've invoked the holy name of national security to get in here to talk to me and with a dog to boot. Now, was my adjutant right or wrong in that statement, gentlemen?"

"That's correct, General," Cal said. "I appreciate you—"

The general cut him off with an upraised hand. "Why don't you just cut straight to it? Now, while you don't look like typical Washington weenies, I sure as hell don't appreciate strangers coming onto my base, right smack dab in the middle of a potential international crisis."

Cal nodded and chose his words wisely, carefully.

"Two Djibouti nationals just entered your camp, General. I'm not sure if you had a chance to speak with them, but we would very much like that opportunity."

The general seemed to be only half listening, because he had suddenly taken a keen interest in Daniel.

"Do I know you, son?" the general asked, meaning Daniel, of course.

"We have met once before, General," Daniel said. The general's eyes flickered with recognition.

"Well I'll be goddamned," the general said, "Snake Eyes, isn't it?"

"Yes, sir."

The general slapped his desk, pointing at Briggs. "I can see by that ponytail that you're not in the Corps anymore. I never did hear what happened to you. Did you get out and secure some fancy job with these two gentlemen?"

"Something like that," Daniel answered with a smile. "My friend here," Daniel pointed to Cal, "is a Marine, too."

The general looked at Cal.

"I know I shouldn't be asking this, but what's your name, son?"

"Stokes, General. Cal Stokes."

The general thought about that for a moment and then

asked, "You wouldn't happen to be related to *Colonel* Stokes, would you?"

"He was my father, General."

The older man nodded. "I'm sorry for your loss, son. I didn't know your father personally, but I knew *of* him, and I suspect you already know that he was *the* Marine's marine."

Cal felt that familiar pit of hollowness deep in his stomach, and after a brief silence, the general changed the subject.

"Well, now that I know that Washington hasn't thrown a trio of spies into my midst, why don't you Marines tell me what you need with those Djibouti nationals?"

Cal nodded for Daniel to explain.

"We're looking for some people, General. Our operation, if you could even call it that, isn't classified or logged in any book, if you take my meaning." The general nodded. "It's possible that these two visitors know the whereabouts of our missing companions."

"Would these missing companions, as you describe them, in any way be linked to the current hubbub between China and Djibouti?" None of the three answered, but the general took their meaning once again. "Gentlemen, I believe it would be best for all of us if we ended this conversation."

"But, General—" Cal said before receiving the raised hand.

"I will not discuss this further, and I suggest you take my lead, unless we all want to be dragged in front of some international tribunal. Now, it was a pleasure meeting you all, but I really do have a pressing schedule to get back to."

Cal was going to protest, but Daniel grabbed his arm and pushed him towards the door.

Once they were outside the office, Cal said, "He knows something. We were so close."

They ignored the curious onlookers as they made their way through the headquarters building and finally found the exit. Just as Daniel was reaching for the doorknob, somebody called from behind.

"Excuse me!" It was a fair-skinned captain, the general's adjutant. He held up a piece of folded paper for Cal. "Gentlemen, the general said you forgot this in his office." Once the piece of paper had changed hands, the peppy adjutant did an about-face and went back to his tasks.

Cal unfolded the paper and read,

The two visitors you are looking for are in the temporary lodging. Get them out of here as soon as you can.

He handed the piece of paper to Daniel, and after the sniper had read it, he handed it to Dr. Higgins.

Higgins looked up from the paper. "Well, I'd say we have quite the mystery on our hands."

CHAPTER FOURTEEN

They'd been waiting around all day for word from Sergeant Peabody, and MSgt Trent was starting to get cabin fever.

"Come on, Gaucho, let's take a walk."

His friend looked up from the bed where he'd been watching reruns of *I Love Lucy*. They'd found a comfortable hotel with decent air conditioning, but the only entertainment they had was a flat screen knockoff that had only one working channel. So much for the modern amenities that had been listed on the hotel brochure.

"We should stay here, Top. You remember what Peabody said: 'The streets aren't safe right now,' so I say we just lay low."

Maybe it had something to do with his enormous size, but Trent wasn't good at lying low. He did what he had to, of course, but he'd rather meet a challenge head on than wait for the enemy to come to him.

"Oh, you're just scared," Trent ribbed. "Come on. You're always saying you need some more excitement in your life."

"I was referring to female companionship. Look what we do for a living, Top."

Trent stood up from the armchair, and stretched. "Well, like it or not, I'm leaving. Unless you want me to get lost in this strange city, you'd better accompany me."

Gaucho looked at Trent for a moment, as if he was wondering whether the Marine was messing with him or not. It was obvious that Trent had no intention of sitting back down. Gaucho groaned, and eased his body up off the bed.

"You know, Top, the last time you convinced me to take a stroll in a strange city we got accosted by a couple of Filipino pimps who didn't like the way we were looking at their women."

"That was just a little bit of fun."

They picked a path that would take them down by the water-front. Trent's thinking was that there would be a breeze coming from the ocean. Gaucho had fired back by saying that there had been plenty of breeze coming out of the air conditioner in their hotel room. Trent ignored the comment and kept walking.

There definitely seemed to be more of a military presence on the streets, but they weren't hassling anyone that the pair observed. Most of the soldiers seemed to be bored, resting up against drab olive Humvees, weapons strung casually across their chests.

They'd just passed a row of vendors yelling at each other about stealing customers when he noticed Gaucho's body tense. Trent didn't have to ask what was going on as he doubled back right behind Gaucho when his friend suddenly began talking about forgetting his movie tickets back at the hotel. That was when Trent saw them too, a trio of soldiers leaning against the building, watching them with more than idle curiosity. They didn't even bother looking away.

"I don't like it," Gaucho said when they were finally out of sight. "We should head back to the hotel and be careful about it."

But Trent was curious now, and without any answers from Cal and Daniel, or Gaucho's friend Sgt. Peabody, Trent figured it was time to do something.

"Let's go back," Trent said.

"Are you crazy?"

"I'm a Marine, aren't I? Come on. Let's go."

Gaucho turned around with obvious reluctance, but he set his jaw and followed his friend. The three soldiers weren't where they had left them, but after they made a couple more turns they did catch sight of them.

The soldiers had taken up a casual walk, maybe fifty feet behind Trent and Gaucho, once again making no attempt to stay hidden. Trent had been in enough cities to understand the general layout, to know that all mazes have their certain commonalities, so he took his time like he was just taking a casual stroll through a new town. He established the persona of the country mouse coming to the city for the first time. He was all wide-eyed and ogling the sights. He finally convinced Gaucho to start talking again, and the two slipped into an easy conversation talking nonsense about the pretty buildings and the wonderful smell of the food coming out of the restaurants.

It wasn't long before Trent found exactly what he was looking for, and he took a sharp right turn after a shawarma café.

"It's a dead end, Top," Gaucho hissed as they entered the long alleyway.

"Come on. I've got something to show you," Trent said excitedly, now hurrying his steps for the first time. When they got to the end of the alleyway, Trent slapped the concrete wall and said, "Oops, my bad!"

When he turned to make his way back out, there stood

the three soldiers that had been following them. Top walked toward them with an incredulous Gaucho at his side. Trent kept his long limbs loose, trying to appear as nonthreatening as possible, still chatting happily. When the soldiers were ten feet away, he stopped as if he had just noticed them for the first time.

"Oh, hey, there, fellas. Y'all wouldn't by any chance know where I could find a Starbucks, would you?"

None of the three answered the question, but Trent could see that they were gripping their weapons a little bit tighter.

"How about a McDonald's? I guess I could settle for one of them McCafes."

Still no response from the soldiers. He looked down at Gaucho. "Well, I guess we'll just have to go find it ourselves," he said sadly. That's when the three rifles came up.

"You are wanted for questioning," the middle man said.

"Who, me?" Trent asked in mock surprise.

"You are wanted for questioning," the soldier repeated.

"Well, I'll be. You know, my travel agent didn't tell me that we were going to have a welcoming party when we got to Djibouti City. Did they tell you?" he asked Gaucho.

Gaucho shook his head, but kept his eyes locked on the three soldiers.

"Well, I hate to tell you this, gentlemen," Trent said, "but I've got a date with a latte, and neither heaven nor hell will keep me from breaking that engagement. So if you'll excuse us —"

There was not even a blink from any of the soldiers; they appeared unaffected by Trent's tactics.

"Ah, I know what this must be about." Trent grabbed Gaucho's hand. "You think that because we're American, we're on a date or something. Is that it?"

Stone-faced stares from the soldiers was the response. They did not appear amused.

"Well," Trent continued, "I've got to admit, you three are some crack detectives, because you got us. You really caught us red-handed. We were just going to go to a local establishment and do a little dancing. But since y'all said that we need to come in for questioning, y'all wouldn't mind if we got in a little dancing right here, would you?"

Gaucho squeezed his hand as if to ask, "What the hell are you doing?"

Trent squeezed it back hoping that his friend would just stay cool.

"Come on, honey," Trent said to Gaucho, "Let's show them a little *Ring Around the Rosy*."

Finally, recognition registered in Gaucho's eyes, and he reached around and grabbed Trent's other hand. The three soldiers stiffened.

Trent said, "Don't worry, we're not armed. We're not the type, I promise."

Gaucho raised their clasped hands to show their empty waistbands.

"Now, here we go. Are you boys watching? *Ring around the rosy, pocketful of posies*," Trent sang as he and Gaucho started to turn slowly, gradually increasing their speed as Trent continued singing. He spied, out of the corner of his eyes, the three soldiers were watching, but he wasn't sure if they were mesmerized or incredulous. Trent kept singing and the dynamic duo kept twirling.

"Ring around the rosy, pocketful of posies."

Trent squeezed Gaucho's hands hard and his friend hung on. The huge Marine took three more hard planted steps and suddenly Gaucho was airborne. Trent flung him with all his might toward the three soldiers who, as Trent expected, raised their muzzles to the sky to block the incoming missile. Gaucho slammed into them, and there were yelps from the downed soldiers. Trent was quick to pounce, slamming one in the nose with his left fist, quickly followed by knocking the other one in the temple with his right elbow. Gaucho had already taken out the third. The two friends rose to admire their handiwork.

Trent motioned down the alley and said, "Why don't we drag these boys out behind that dumpster over there? I'd love to know what they have to say about this mysterious general who's hell-bent on kicking America's ass."

They dragged the three bodies to the end of the alley and waited for them to regain consciousness.

CHAPTER FIFTEEN

The interrogation had been short, but fruitful. Top and Gaucho learned that the three soldiers weren't soldiers at all. Only one man could actually speak English, thus the most MSgt Trent could gather was that the three men were some kind of low-level militia. Thus they knew how to take orders, and that's what they'd been doing. They'd been paid to put on the uniforms in order to augment the military presence on the streets of Djibouti City. A bonus had been promised for every foreign military-looking man brought in. Priority was given to English speakers. Top and Gaucho had just been in the right place at the right time.

Top might have felt bad for them except earlier in the day he was standing on the wrong end of an automatic weapon. At least now he felt like things were going somewhere. They didn't have a name, but they did have a location. The English-speaking man in uniform had described it as a warehouse or storage facility that was serving as their assigned center of operations.

After they'd gotten what information they could from the fake soldiers, MSgt Trent ordered them to strip down to their underwear. Using the men's handcuffs and gagging them with their T-shirts, they were restrained.

Top tossed the restrained men into the dumpster and told them to be quiet. Then he promised that they would return to release them out of the makeshift cell, but only if the captors behaved. While Top would have loved to take the weapons with them, there was no way they could carry them inconspicuously on the streets. So he ejected the magazines and rounds in the chambers and tossed the weapons into the dumpster. They took the ammunition, of course, and deposited it in various trash cans on their way to the warehouse.

"You think it's a good idea to leave them back there?" Gaucho asked as they left the alleyway.

"Not much else we could do with them. As Gunny Highway used to say, "We must improvise, adapt, and overcome."

Gaucho shook his head. "How come you Marines have so many one-liners?"

Top grinned down at his friend. "Oh, you know, it's just practice for when we steal all the pretty girls from you dog-faced Hoo-ahs."

Gaucho rolled his eyes and they walked on.

It was getting darker now, but in MSgt Trent's estimation the temperature hadn't dropped a single degree.

They kept going until they reached the roughest section of the city that they'd visited yet. There were more curious glances now because the ranks of the foreigners had thinned out blocks before.

"What's your plan, Kemo Sabe?" Gaucho asked. "Just you and me against the world?"

"Naw, I thought that maybe we could play like door-to-door salesmen. What do you think we should sell, encyclopedias or those knives that you never have to sharpen again?"

"You're kidding, right?"

"I guess you'll just have to wait and see." Then, after Gaucho had a moment to digest that morsel, Trent said, "But seriously though, let's play this by ear, get eyes on, and see what we can find out. I mean, if they'd really wanted to do us some harm, they would've shot us."

"Is that what that whole *Ring Around the Rosy* thing was about? I know you Marines are crazy and all, but that one took the cake, Top."

"Just don't go around saying it was your idea, Hombre."

"You don't have to worry about that. Nobody would believe me anyway."

Top was about to reply when Gaucho pointed with a motion of his head.

"That looks like the spot."

It matched the description the soldier had given. The only problem was, there didn't seem to be any activity occurring around the rusted out building. They did one full loop around the property, half expecting to be ambushed by a platoon at any point. The only person they encountered was a little old lady with gray hair that cascaded down her chest, mumbling to herself as she shuffled along. She didn't seem to notice them so they walked on. There was a small truck court on the other side, but the only thing it contained was an old two-wheeled beater up on concrete blocks.

"Place looks deserted," Gaucho said. "You think they told the truth?"

Top shrugged. "Maybe, anything's possible. I believe those boys believed they were telling the truth."

"Yeah, I think you're right."

"Well, I've taken it up to this point. What do you think we should do?" Top asked.

"Since we're here, why don't we take a look inside? That

door on the other side shouldn't be too hard to jimmy open," Gaucho said, motioning back the way they'd come.

"See? I knew you'd find your sea legs."

As they made their way closer to the door, there was still no noise. The night suddenly felt eerily quiet, and Top wondered if he should call his friend off. Gaucho was already examining the lock on the weather-beaten door when the skin on the back of his neck started to tingle. He looked in every direction, but didn't see anybody watching. He was just about to ask Gaucho if he was feeling the same tingling sensation when off to the side someone said, "Psst."

Both of them snapped their heads in that direction; it was the little old woman with the white stringy hair.

"You think she's talking to us?" Trent inquired.

"Who else?" Gaucho whispered.

"Psst," the old woman said again, this time motioning with her hand for them to come over.

"It could be a trap," Gaucho said.

"Come on man, she's just a little old lady. You think they'd put her out here to lure in unsuspecting Americans? Maybe she's seen something. Let's go talk to her."

Trent waved back to the old woman, who shuffled backwards into the shadows, almost but not completely disappearing into the gloom. When they reached the small alcove, the woman was waiting, her hands clasped in front of her.

"Ma'am, can we help you with something?" Trent asked politely.

The woman didn't say anything, her face obscured by her hair. Without saying anything, she was starting to give Top the creeps.

"We should go," Gaucho insisted.

The old woman's head turned. She must've been taking in both men behind that curtain of hair.

"Didn't anyone teach you not to talk to strangers?" the woman asked in a low Southern drawl.

"You son of a—Peabody, is that you?" Trent asked.

The old woman's hands reached up, parted her curtain of hair, revealing Sergeant Elliot Peabody's grinning face.

"Surprise, ladies," he said.

Top was at a loss for words. First the shifty character he'd met at the hotel and now the old woman – he felt he was losing his tactically trained mind.

Peabody answered his unasked question. "Didn't Gaucho tell you that I was a drama major at NYU?" He stood up to his full height and bowed regally. "Thanks to the powers that be, now I get to act full time. You want to tell me what you two are doing here?"

"Same thing as you," Gaucho said.

"How did you find this place? I had to spend close to twenty grand just to get into the neighborhood."

Gaucho pointed to Trent, and Trent quickly explained what had happened with the three soldiers. Peabody let out a low whistle.

"Hey diddle diddle, right up the middle. Isn't that what they say in the Corps, Top?"

"You got it."

"Well, those crack troops were only half right. Your timing's pretty good though; I was about to call to give you an update. Here's the deal: This building is just a temporary collection point. From what I've gathered, they've got a couple of these scattered around the city. This is the only one I've personally had eyes on, but I've got some friends watching the others. Same deal with each building. They bring in people, two to three at a time, for questioning, but they never really question them. They just load them on a bus and when there's enough to go, they take the bus to a different locale."

"Where does the bus go?" Gaucho asked.

"I was just getting to that, if you'd let me continue," Peabody stated in mock annoyance. "Turns out that someone's established a hasty army campground just outside the city. As it was described to me, it looks more like a POW camp, so my best guess is that that's where they're doing their "questioning." It all seems to be pretty cordial. No fights that I've seen, and everybody came pretty willingly. But the compliance was mostly due to the guns pointed at their backs."

"But why round up foreigners?" Top asked. "They've got to know word's going to get out, and the Djibouti government's going to have ambassadors breathing down their necks."

"I've had some time to ruminate on that question," Peabody said. "Shuffling up and down this street will give you time to do that, and the best I can figure is this is a preemptive strike. What if they're just clearing the streets of suspected operators like us so they can get about their business without worrying about someone messing with their plans from the inside?"

"Couldn't they just declare martial law or establish a curfew?"

"Sure, but that wouldn't give them real control. Just think about it. If you were about to pick a fight with the biggest dog in the yard, wouldn't you rather have that dog's puppies held on the sidelines as insurance, just in case?"

Trent wasn't buying it. It sounded like a whole lot of hassle with very little reward.

"Listen," Peabody continued. "I don't know who you all really work for, but I suggest you all watch your backs."

"What do you mean by that?" Gaucho asked.

"I've got a bad feeling about this one. You know when you

think you're doing the right thing, but you're convinced that someone is manipulating your actions?"

"Do you think the CIA is in on this?"

"I didn't say that. What I *did say* is there are powers in play that we might not even know about, and we all need to be careful."

"Roger that," Trent said, taking a step back in his mind. He was, as if on a chess board, mentally arranging the figures he knew to be in play. They included the mysterious general, likely the Djibouti government, the US, and maybe even the Chinese. Top didn't know what it all meant, but he knew how Peabody felt. The situation was like a cauldron of hot water; it kept getting hotter and was about to boil over. That's the feeling he'd had all day but hadn't been able to pinpoint until that very moment.

"Okay then," he said. "What's our next move?"

Before Sergeant Peabody could answer, four quick shots rang out from the end of the street, and Top felt rounds fly by. When he turned to ask Gaucho if he was okay, he saw that his friend was looking at the ground. Top's eyes followed Gaucho's gaze, even while trying to pinpoint exactly where the shots had come from. Sergeant Peabody was laying on his back, the old woman's hair parted neatly down the middle. His eyes were wide open, and it was obvious he was dead.

"Jesus," Gaucho said.

Trend didn't think; he just moved. He scooped up the thin, lifeless body and threw Peabody over his shoulder.

Without any other options, Top and Gaucho did all they could do; they ran for their lives.

CHAPTER SIXTEEN

The transient housing turned out to be rows of shipping containers converted into housing units. There was a strip of masking tape on most of the doors indicating exactly who was occupying each air-conditioned unit. *Gonzales*. *Davis*. *LeFleur* with the "F" crossed out and rewritten. They kept looking until they found one marked *Guests x 2*.

Cal knocked on the metal hatch. A kid with an unbuttoned shirt answered the door. He looked like he'd just awakened from a deep sleep. He rubbed his eyes and asked, "Yes?"

"I'm sorry to bother you," Cal apologized, "but we were wondering if we could talk to you and your friend."

After a moment's hesitation, as the kid pondered a mental list of reasons to not allow the Americans in, the boy nodded, motioning them inside. The interior of the shipping container included a set of bunk beds, a two chests of drawers, and some empty foot lockers with the lids propped open.

There was a tight-skinned older man lying down on the bottom cot. He sat up as the four entered. The boy said something to the old man and the old man nodded.

"He understands English," the boy said, "but he doesn't speak it very well. My name is Christian and he's my grandfather."

"I'm Cal, and that's Dr. Higgins, Daniel, and this is Liberty."

Christian looked down at the dog and, obviously, hadn't noticed her before. "Can I pet her?" he asked, bending down and kneeling before Cal could answer, "Sure."

Liberty was cautious at first but after a few strokes on her head, she curled in close to the boy.

"This might seem like a strange question," Cal began, "but you may have met with two of our friends."

"Here on the base?"

"No, out there."

The boy looked up from his kneeling position. His eyes were cautious now. "Who are your friends?"

He'd discussed with Daniel and Dr. Higgins about how much they should divulge. They had no idea who these two strangers were. For all they knew they could be some locals trying to take advantage of the situation. They might have even had something to do with the plane being shot down, and now that Cal thought about it, who better to send in to do the negotiating than a kid and an old man? They would not appear to pose a threat and were sure to be let in.

It was actually Dr. Higgins who answered first, stepping forward. "Christian, their names are Vince and Karl, and we believe they are in grave danger."

The boy stood and Cal sensed the kid recalled the names. "How do you know them?" Christian asked.

Smart kid. Don't give away too much too soon.

The kid looked like he was going to clam up, but the grandfather walked forward, placed a hand on his grandson's shoulder and said something. There was a brief exchange, and Christian turned back to them.

"My grandfather says we should trust you."

"That's completely up to you," said Dr. Higgins, "But why does your grandfather think you should trust us?"

Christian's face scrunched up like he was trying to find the right words. "My grandfather, well, he has certain insights that he's tried to explain to me, but I don't completely understand. People come to him when they need things."

"Is he an elder of some sort?"

"The closest word I can come up with in English is Shaman but that's not really what he is, at least that's not what I believe he is. He doesn't do magic, at least not that I've seen."

Dr. Higgins nodded like it was all such a natural thing. Daniel didn't seem concerned either, but then again, Daniel had the same sort of insights that Christian's grandfather seemed to have. It only seemed bizarre to Cal; he preferring living and thinking in black and white.

"Did you see Vince and Karl? Did you see what happened to them?"

Christian nodded. "We spent two days with them." And then with a pained face, he went on to explain everything that had happened, from the surprise introduction at the small hut right up to when Vince and Karl were captured and taken away.

Daniel asked, "Why didn't they take you two?"

The boy looked at his grandfather and then back at Daniel. "As I told you, my grandfather is a special man. He commands a certain respect amongst our people. The Asian man wanted them to take us. He said we were a threat as well, but the soldiers wouldn't allow it. They thought my grandfather would put some kind of curse on them."

The grandfather nodded to accentuate the point, like he actually would do such a thing. Then he said something to Christian, who nodded and added, "My grandfather is the president's uncle. My grandfather now believes when the Asian man became aware of my grandfather's stature and connection to the president, he decided not to press for our capture. There are strange things happening here, Mr. Cal, and my grandfather and I would like to help if you will allow us."

They didn't have much to go on, but the help of a relative of the Djibouti president might come in handy. Hell, if they really got in a bind maybe the old man could cast a spell of protection on them.

"The first thing we need to do is get off this base. Do you guys know of any place we can stay in town?" Cal asked.

"I have some friends who could help not far from here."

"Okay, let's go. Do you need any help with your things?"

Christian pointed to the backpack on the floor. "That's all we have."

They left quickly. Cal was concerned about the commanding officer's warning. *What had it meant?*

They'd just passed through the front gate when one of the guards warned them, "If you're leaving, know you will not be getting back here for a while."

"Why's that?" Daniel queried.

"Didn't you hear? They just put us on lockdown," the guard responded.

"Why?"

"I don't know. Way above my pay grade, Mister. But if I were you, I'd hightail it to wherever you're headed. Keep your heads down until you arrive at your destination."

CHAPTER SEVENTEEN

Trent and Gaucho somehow made it back to their hotel alive. They bounced from shadow to shadow for what seemed like hours, and Trent carried Sergeant Peabody's lifeless form the entire way.

The streets were empty now, and every building seemed to have its interior lights turned off. In stark contrast the street lamps seemed to be brighter than usual. They may have appeared brighter because no light emanated from the houses. Then again, it could have been just in their heads since they were trying to avoid capture.

When they arrived at their hotel, the front door was locked. Gaucho peered inside, attracting the man at the front desk. He sauntered over to them, unlocking the door, casually holding a shotgun in his hands. He let them in without asking any questions, although he did look at the body Trent was carrying with mild curiosity. After taking a moment to stare at the body, he pointed with his thumb back toward the bar.

The bar itself was only illuminated by a couple of candles, and Gaucho had the distinct feeling of having stepped back in time. Then he noticed the wounded. They were lying on the rows of couches that someone had brought down from the rooms.

A woman looked up from where she was tending one of the wounded and inquired about Sgt. Peabody, "How bad is he hurt?"

"He's dead," Gaucho declared, sorrow lacing those definitive words.

The woman blinked once, nodded, and then said, "I'm sorry. You can put him over here if you'd like."

She pointed to the far corner, where sheets were laid out on the floor like someone had expected the dead to come and be triaged. After laying Sgt. Peabody on one of the sheets and covering him up with another, Gaucho and Top returned to the woman who seemed to be in charge of the makeshift First Aid station. She was providing a shot of some dark liquid to one of her patients, and the man winced as he drank it.

"I wish I had something else for you, but that will help you relax," she was saying.

The man nodded and then he closed his eyes. She stood up and spoke to Gaucho and Trent.

"You're welcome to have some if you like," she said, meaning the bar. "The owner says it's on the house."

"Well that's nice of him," Gaucho said sarcastically. The woman looked like she was going to say something, but didn't.

Then she asked, "How did your friend die?"

"He was shot."

She thought about that for a moment. Gaucho thought she had a very striking face, like someone who used to model because their nose was angled in just the right direction.

"We haven't seen any gunshot victims as of yet, so far only people that had been beaten. However, I'm sure they'll come soon enough. Are either of you injured?"

"Just some bumps and scrapes, Ma'am," Trent said, "We'll be fine."

"Regardless, you should let me take a look at them."

"Are you a doctor?" Gaucho asked.

"I'm a nurse. My husband works at the State Department, and I was just in town to meet an old friend for a drink."

"You picked some time to go out for a drink."

"Well, I didn't know they were planning on declaring martial law."

"Is that what happened?" Trent asked.

The woman shrugged. "No one knows what is happening. One minute our lives were normal. The next minute our cell phones didn't work, TV stations were no longer broadcasting, and the only ones with any ability to communicate are the soldiers patrolling our streets."

"What about your husband? Have you been able to get in touch with him?"

"Not yet. But he knows I can take care of myself. This isn't our first time in this type of situation."

"Were you in the army?" Gaucho asked.

"No. We've just had the good fortune of being posted to some of the world's best war torn metropolises. And here we thought Djibouti was on its way up," she laughed, "Maybe it's us? Maybe we're the bad luck?"

Gaucho thanked the woman, and informed her they'd be back after cleaning themselves up - the shower was calling. Trent needed it the most since the majority of his shirt and cheek was covered with Sgt. Peabody's blood. They went up to their room to freshen up.

Gaucho had just finished toweling off when he heard the *pop, pop, pop* of gunfire in the distance. He went to the window, half expecting to see pins of light. All he saw were the empty streets of Djibouti City. There were more sounds of gunfire followed by silence.

"That's been going on ever since you got in the shower," Trent said from where he was sitting in the leather armchair, trying to get a signal on his cell phone.

"We need to get hold of Cal. You think we can figure out a way to patch through Charlottesville?"

"I'm sure Neil's working on it," Trent replied.

Now it was Gaucho's turn to feel antsy. After seeing Elliot Peabody killed, he needed to do something. But what? They were stuck in the middle of a city in lockdown with little more than pistols and a couple of wads of cash.

"Do you think we can get over to the embassy?" Gaucho wondered, aloud.

"I'm sure they've got that place surrounded."

Trent was right. Then Gaucho had an idea. It was a crazy idea, but—well, their options were limited. He told Trent what he was thinking, and Trent's eyes went wide.

"And you were the one calling me nutso? Boy, we better have your head checked out once we get home."

"C'mon, man. What else have we got?"

"All right, fine. But if this thing goes south—"

He didn't have to finish his thoughts. The implications were obvious. If it went wrong, they'd be dead. But Gaucho had never been in the business of playing it safe. He'd escaped his family's checkered past and then served in the most elite special forces unit in the world.

To stack even more chips in his favor, he had his best friend, Marine MSgt Willy Trent on his side, and in Gaucho's mind there wasn't anything the two couldn't accomplish together, the Dynamic Duo.

CHAPTER EIGHTEEN

President Zimmer had met with the president of the Republic of Djibouti on several occasions. The man was friendly and, like President Zimmer, came from a long line of diplomats. He was a cosmopolitan and well-educated man, but Zimmer wouldn't necessarily call him a staunch ally. During his short time in office, Zimmer figured they'd established a good working relationship.

It didn't hurt that the US military presence in Djibouti deterred any of their past enemies from making a play on Djibouti's strategic location. As the only permanent U.S. base on the African continent, the Republic of Djibouti was important for the United States as a whole, and for Zimmer specifically. So when the president's secretary said she was having a hard time getting the president of Djibouti on the phone, Zimmer was more than a little concerned.

Reports were leaking out, and he'd already talked to the chairman of the Joint Chiefs of Staff regarding the lockdown status of Camp Lemonnier. He had pressed the CIA for information, but even they admitted any analysis, at this point, was mere speculation because rumors were running rampant at the US embassy in Djibouti. To make matters worse, he was suddenly unable to get hold of his own man on the ground, Cal Stokes. While he had first been annoyed that Cal had done an end run around his plans, Zimmer acknowledged that as the situation on the ground had deteriorated, Cal's instincts were correct. Now that he'd had a moment to think about it, why had he tried to stop Cal and his team from going to Djibouti?

When the answer arrived, it was an uncomfortable one. Plain and simple, President Brandon Zimmer had tried to protect his own ass. It was an election year, and although no one had yet risen to challenge him personally, and the polls generally said he was an overwhelming favorite, he'd already seen what news stories could do to sway the public opinion. The governor of Texas had been caught completely unaware, and while he wasn't sure if Tony McKnight's camp was behind the incident, President Zimmer could appreciate the fact that the congressman would take advantage of a flailing opponent. That defined politics after all — taking advantage when you could and watching your back at every step.

He envied Cal and Daniel. They lived in a world where it was much easier to separate right from wrong. Not for the first time, he questioned his decision to enter the political realm. It was like a constant race to the bottom, hooking and jabbing, trying to get a leg up on the competition, while simultaneously attempting to both appear as the good guy and represent one's constituents. If the gold medal was the pinnacle of achievement at the Olympics, the United States presidency was like standing on the right hand of God in politics.

While he chided himself for his hypervigilance, he understood it was a necessary precaution. Even now there was a very real worry that the lead element of The Jefferson Group might be found and exposed. They were good, if not the best, but they were still human. And with Djibouti in seeming upheaval anything was possible.

"Mr. President, I have the president of Djibouti on the line," his secretary's voice came over the speaker phone.

"Thank you, Betty." He picked up the receiver. He hated talking over the speakerphone.

"I'm sorry to have kept you waiting, Mr. President," came the staticky voice of his foreign counterpart.

"No need to apologize," Zimmer replied. "I understand you're having some problems, and I wanted to call to see if we could be of any assistance."

There was more static, and Zimmer wondered if his ally was searching for the right words or if the connection was really that bad.

"I'm sorry, Mr. President," came the staticky voice again. "They tell me the connection is horrid. We may only have a moment. As you have probably heard a curfew has been established in our capital city. I'm not yet aware of any fatalities, but there have been injuries, I am sorry to say."

Zimmer could have asked a laundry list of questions but he waited, providing the Djibouti president time through the bad connection to relay the information he needed to share. "I don't know how else to say this, so pardon my bluntness. My advisors believe there will be an attempt to remove me from power. As of yet, we do not know who the leader of the opposition is, but we are fairly certain that someone within the military is behind the coup."

There was shouting in the background now. Zimmer asked, "Is everything okay? Are you safe?"

The shouting continued, but his voice was calm when he replied. "They are trying to force their way into my safe house. Do not worry. I am surrounded by loyal men. It may seem melodramatic for me to say, but my life is of no consequence. I would gladly die for my country, Mr. President. But

I must warn you that there are other powers at play that—well, I'm sorry to say I may have played into their hands."

A fresh wave of static hit the connection now, and Zimmer could only hear fractured words from the Djibouti president.

"Are you there? Are you still there?" Zimmer exclaimed. Then the line went dead. President Zimmer waited a moment before calling for his secretary. "Betty, can you get him back on the line, please?"

"I have him on line two," she said. The connection clicked over again. There was more static and more shouting.

"Mr. President, are you there?"

"Yes, I'm here," Zimmer answered.

"Your men. I wanted to tell you that they have your men." His voice was hurried now, almost panicked.

"Which men? Which men do they have?"

"The ones they captured when they blew up the plane."

At least it wasn't Cal, but it was finally confirmation that Vince and Karl had been captured.

"Tell me who has them."

"I—" There was lots of crackling static now. It sounded like he was saying that he was sorry, but Zimmer couldn't tell with the connection so bad. Like before, it clicked off, and his secretary came on the line again.

"I'm sorry, Mr. President. I've lost him. I will see if the Signal Corp can reestablish the connection."

Zimmer almost told her not to bother, but instead he said, "Thank you."

Now it seemed that the president's worst fears were coming to fruition. Whoever was behind the coup held hostage the two Delta operators. America could quite possibly be getting ready to receive a huge hit to its credibility. To make matters even worse, the Chinese were in play. They'd had something to do with it, and that made trying to predict what that communist government would do almost impossible.

He had to face the facts; it was his fault. If there was anything that he'd learned from Cal and his friends, it was that a good leader was always accountable and never shirked that responsibility, regardless how trying the times. Like the Djibouti president, he had to face the fire. Now wasn't the time to hide behind the shield of his office. Good men were out there; his men were out there, and he needed to help them. He couldn't do that by sending a protest to the U.N. or by ushering diplomats to the Chinese embassy.

Damn the election year, he thought. If it was his time then it was his time. Just like his embattled ally had just said, President Zimmer knew that he would die for his country. In his case that probably meant a political death, not a physical one. As he stared out the Oval Office window, he made his decision.

"Betty, get me the chairman of the Joint Chiefs of Staff, the Director of the CIA, the Vice President, and Congressman McKnight on the telephone."

It took almost ten minutes for all four men to get on secure lines. The president, without greeting the men, began delegating orders.

"General, I would like you and the CIA to provide me with a joint analysis regarding the current situation in Djibouti. How long do you think that will take?"

"My people are on it now, sir. I'd say we can provide the analysis within the hour."

"Mr. Director?" the president asked.

"Yes, I think we can make that happen, Mr. President."

"Congressman McKnight, I know you're probably neck deep in the primaries right now, but I need your assistance."

"Anything, Mr. President," McKnight said.

"As my closest ally on the Republican side of the aisle, I

was hoping you would help me settle the House Republicans with what's going to occur."

"I don't understand, sir. Has something happened?"

"I'll get to that in a moment, Tony."

"Vice President Southgate," the president said, "I need you to return to Washington to help coordinate things for me here."

"Yes, Mr. President. But if I can ask, where are you going?"

"I guess there's no time left," President Zimmer mused aloud. "Gentlemen, I'm going to retrieve some friends who I put in a very precarious position, and I assume full responsibility. I—" There was silence from the others as they waited for the president to complete his announcement. "Gentleman, consider the following classified Top Secret Presidential. In fifteen minutes I depart the White House for Andrews Air Force Base. I want you to know I did not come to this decision lightly but this is the right thing to do. For once I feel like doing absolutely the right thing."

"Mr. President, maybe we should speak about this before —so—," Vice President Southgate tried to interject.

The president spoke over him, "I'm flying to Djibouti within the hour. I expect your reports by the time I am airborne. I'll relay follow-on instructions on the way there. Now if you'll excuse me, gentlemen, I have a plane to catch."

CHAPTER NINETEEN

It took Congressman McKnight exactly thirty-one minutes to make his decision. This opportunity could be gone in the blink of an eye; it was one of those crucial moments he knew he'd never get again. He didn't really have an explanation for his actions. At face value, there didn't seem to be much future reward in the act, but McKnight believed offerings should come in small doses. It was better to give a little at a time, rather than giving away the farm in one fell swoop.

And yet, he struggled. Ever since declaring that he was going to run for president, he'd made it a habit to time himself every time he made an important decision. Prior to today, the longest it had taken him was nine minutes, so for the congressman, thirty-one minutes stretched out like eternity.

He'd often wondered how long it had taken important men to make important decisions. In history's hindsight, wasn't it really the critical decisions that made the man? How long had it taken President Harry Truman to decide that he was going to drop the atomic bomb on Japan? How much time did it take Adolf Hitler to determine he needed to annihilate the Jews?

McKnight's decision might not have seemed so earth shattering, but deep down he knew this was a decision that would either haunt him forever as an epic failure, or shoot him into the political stratosphere. When left to ponder those pros and cons, he decided to bet on himself.

Besides the coded message he sent was indecipherable. It was so every day common that no one could twist it. His secret was safe.

The world would soon know what President Zimmer was, and that was without McKnight's help. There were others who might be curious, if not concerned, about Zimmer's impromptu actions. So off the anonymous message flew - first to McKnight's moneyman, and then it would be passed off through the series of buffers that would scrub the cyber trail clean.

———

It was the men on the receiving end of McKnight's message who made the real decisions. Would the information be worth their time? It was those decision makers who soon began moving the chess pieces across the board. Those decision makers were in it for the long game. If this tiny distraction didn't work out, it didn't matter. No time would be lost, and no one would be the wiser.

But, if there was even the slightest chance of getting a step up on the American president, they figured it was well worth the risk. After all, it wasn't them on the ground, and it wasn't technically their people. Whatever came back pointed in their direction they could easily deny. But if they gambled on that minuscule probability, they would watch and wait patiently as they had for many years. By the time the information filtered its way into Djibouti, contingency plans had already been formulated.

CHAPTER TWENTY

Although the distance from their hotel to either Camp Lemonnier or the embassy was essentially the same, MSgt Trent figured their chances of accessing the embassy were better. He believed because the entire city was on a curfew and communications block, the base would probably be on lockdown. If that were the case, so would the embassy. That presented a problem. While Camp Lemonnier might have seemed the obvious choice because of his and Gaucho's military service, it didn't necessarily guarantee they would be granted entry.

Sure, they could go up to the main gate and flash their ID cards, but Top and Gaucho agreed it was better to take a risk outside the front doors of the embassy because of its status as a safe haven. And as a sliver of sovereign US soil, they should be allowed inside, as long as they could get there. That was the tricky part.

They snaked their way through the streets without detection. It had taken them over an hour to locate the assets they required. There just weren't many men that were as tall as Trent. The soldier they finally did settle on was a good six inches shorter than Trent, but he was a heavy man. Thus, the issued uniform had been larger in order to accommodate the man's extra girth, but the arms and legs were still long and had to be rolled to fit the current wearer. For Top, they were an almost perfect fit.

They ditched the fat soldier and his companion not far from the hotel. They were tied together nut to butt. Other than headaches when they awoke, they would be no worse for wear when they were found hours later.

The part of the whole scheme Gaucho resisted was the cuffs. They looked like a relic from the first World War, and when they didn't immediately lock into place, he wondered if they'd be able to ever get them off.

"You just sit back there and relax, Gaucho," Top said, putting the Humvee in drive and pulling away from its former home as an impromptu roadblock.

"Do you really think this'll work?"

"There's always a chance we'll be shot, of course. I'd say we've got a sixty-forty chance of getting into the embassy, but let's not talk about that. Let's talk about why my Latin little brother isn't his normal cheery self."

"Well, let's see, maybe it has something to do with the fact that I'm pretending to be a prisoner right now, and we have no idea as to the location or status of our friends. Oh yeah, and we can't even use a cell phone to request assistance. And the cherry on top is we just witnessed my friend, Sergeant Peabody, get killed before our eyes."

Top's smile disappeared. "I'm sorry about Peabody; I really am, Gaucho. But to survive, we've got to look past all of that. You know how this works. If we start second guessing ourselves, who knows what hell we're gonna catch."

"I know, and it's not that I blame myself, or anything we did, for what happened, but I just can't shake what Peabody said."

"Which part?" Top queried.

"The part where he said we better watch our backs, that there's other stuff going on in the wings that we don't know about yet."

"Yeah, I've been thinking about that, too. What do you think he meant?"

"I guess we'll find out, won't we?" Then Gaucho forced a smile, "Come on, Top, let's see if we can't cheat death again."

The trick was to pretend that you belonged, and that's exactly what Top did. The good news was that there was no traffic on the streets. The bad news was the only traffic were military vehicles, but it was easy enough for him to mimic whatever motions the other passing Humvee drivers made. A nod here. A curt wave there. Miraculously, no one stopped them.

"See, I told you that this was going to be easy," Top said as they cruised along.

"We're not there yet."

"And here I thought your attitude had just turned a corner."

And just as they did turn a corner, the United States Embassy came into view. Whatever relief they felt was quickly stripped away when they saw what they faced. A semicircle of military vehicles, machine guns mounted in the beds, had cordoned off the street and main gate leading to their target.

At first Top thought, or rather hoped, that they were security forces on the American payroll. But his hopes were dashed as they neared the embassy.

"Okay, then," Trent said, "We knew this was a probability, so let's just take it slow and hope that none of these idiots gets a happy trigger finger."

Top eased the Humvee up to the first vehicle, and he noted the Marine sentries atop the embassy building. A serious-looking character stepped out of an armored vehicle and headed their way. He asked Top something in Arabic which, of course, he didn't understand so he decided to improvise.

In his best accented English, he said, "Did they not tell you? We must speak English."

"I had not heard," the surprised soldier said in English that sounded better than Top's. "I will pass the word to my men." He looked past Top into the backseat. "Who is this?"

"Prisoner for trade with the Americans. General's orders."

Apparently whoever this general was, he demanded the utmost respect of his men because no further questions came forth. The soldier turned and yelled something to his men. Then, remembering the general's alleged orders, he yelled in English for his men to move the trucks aside to let them through.

"Keep your fingers crossed," Trent muttered to Gaucho.

"If you pull this off, drinks are on me for a month," Gaucho promised.

"I'll take two months, thank you very much."

Once the barrier was finally moved, the soldier motioned for them to pass.

"Madre de Dios," Gaucho whispered, "I can't believe you did it."

Top tried to keep a straight face as they rolled past curious eyes following them the entire way. "Here's the tricky part," he said.

They pulled up to the second barricade manned by the United States Marines. One soldier stepped around the barricade and the guy, despite his full combat attire, was all spit and polish. The kid looked like he had jumped off a recruiting poster and spent time as a rifle twirler at 8th and I.

Trent was surprised to see the rank insignia of a Gunnery Sergeant on the Marine's uniform.

"May I help you gentlemen?" the Marine politely asked.

There was no question in MSgt Trent's mind that the young gunny would have no problem signaling to his comrades up on the roof to shoot the blazes out of the Humvee if required.

"Well, gunny, my friend and I were wondering if we might seek asylum in your fine establishment."

A slightly raised eyebrow was the initial response that Top received.

"Am I correct in assuming, sir, that you've commandeered this vehicle and have impersonated yourself as a soldier of the Republic of Djibouti?"

Top could almost hear Gaucho flinch. "That's about the long and short of it, Gunny."

"East coast or west coast?" the Marine questioned.

"Sorry?"

"Hollywood or sand fleas?"

Top finally got the Marine's inference. He was asking where Trent had gone to boot camp. Hollywood for MCRD San Diego and sand fleas for Parris Island.

"Sand fleas, Gunny."

"And your friend back there?"

"Aw, he's harmless. He's just a dirty dogface who is proud to call a United States Marine his best friend."

Top thanked his lucky stars that the Marine Corps chose their best and brightest to become Marines on embassy duty. The gunny standing next to him was no exception. The only thing he wished was that the Marine would move things along.

Top had seen some motion in the ranks behind them and could only assume that the soldier he first talked to had called back to headquarters and was now being told there was no prisoner exchange and, no, he did not have to speak English.

"I assume you gentlemen have identification?"

Trent went to reach in his pocket, but the Marine stopped

him. "Just wait until we get inside. Your friends over there look to be suddenly paying more attention to our little powwow. Let's wait until you're inside, and I can have my Marines give you a full cavity search."

Top didn't doubt it by the gunny's tone, but was more than a little relieved when the Marine called out to the corporal behind the barricade, "Please move it aside."

Top didn't allow himself to breathe sweet relief until he parked the Humvee in a spot labelled GUEST. The barricades closed behind them. He tossed the handcuff keys back to Gaucho who undid them with a little forced effort and disembarked from the vehicle.

"How much trouble am I going to get in for this?" the Gunny asked after he checked their identification.

"None, as far as I'm concerned," Top said. "If anybody gives you a hard time, you just tell them to come talk to me."

The Marine shook his head and actually smiled.

"Top, do you ever find yourself mystified by the fact that there is no place too strange or situation so bizarre that you cannot and will not meet a United States Marine?"

MSgt Trent grinned. "Tell me about it, Gunny."

The good gunny, Gunnery Sergeant Whitaker, found Top a just-too-snug set of workout gym shorts and shirt. He then escorted Gaucho and Top to the CIA head of station located within the embassy.

"Are you sure you wouldn't rather see the ambassador first?" Gunny Whitaker asked.

"We'll visit him next," Gaucho said. "We've got to tell this guy he's a man down."

"I hadn't heard."

"We're the only ones who know," Trent explained.

"If I can ask, Top, who was it?" the Marine implored.

"Elliot Peabody. Did you know him?"

The Marine nodded. "He didn't spend much time around

here, but when he did, he always made the effort to stop by our after-shift poker games. He always won too, although he always gave the money back to the Marines, and I'm sure he gave them a little bit extra, at least that's what I've been told. He sure was a good man. I'm sorry."

"Me too," Gaucho said.

"Well, here we are." The Marine pointed at a door with no visible markings other than a few scratches from use. Gunny Whitaker introduced him to the station chief whose name was Lane Wiley. Wiley didn't get up from his desk nor did he even offer them chairs until Gaucho gruffly announced that they had news concerning Elliot Peabody.

"That will be all. Thank you, Gunnery Sergeant."

The Marine took one last look at Top and Gaucho as if to ask, "*Do you really want me to go?*" But Trent nodded, and the Marine left.

Wiley had the bland look of a man you could meet and forget thirty seconds later. Even his voice sounded like drone monotone. It sounded like a teacher who had been teaching the same lesson for fifty years and along the way lost the gift of inflection.

"Where is Elliot?" Wiley asked. "For three days, he hasn't checked in."

Three days, Gaucho thought, that couldn't be right. "Sorry, did you say *three* days?"

"Not that it's any of your concern, but yes. The longest I let my coworkers go without checking in is two, so you can imagine my concern when two days slipped by, and now it's a third. So let's have it. Where is Elliot?"

The way the man had said coworker instead of subordinate or man struck a wrong chord with Gaucho. *Something was wrong*, Gaucho thought. "Elliot Peabody is dead, Mr. Wiley," Gaucho said readying himself to judge Wiley's reaction.

"I find that very hard to believe. There have been no reports of fatalities in the city, and Elliot is quite an expert at his craft."

Gaucho had to hold himself back from slapping the smug station chief's mouth.

"I'm telling you, he's dead."

It was obvious that the man still didn't believe him.

"So you come in here hoping to catch my ear, concocting this story, for what purpose? For money? Is that what you want? Well good try, gentlemen, but I'm not buying."

Before Gaucho could stop himself, he blurted aloud, "He was my friend, goddammit. And you want to know how I know he died? Because we were right beside him when he was shot. My friend here," he pointed to Top, "carried him two miles after he died."

Now Wiley sat back in his chair and clasped his hands in his lap. "He was your friend, you say. Then how was it that you encountered your *friend* on the streets of Djibouti in the midst of a coup?"

Gaucho had had enough. "We'd like to speak to the ambassador," he said through clenched teeth.

Wiley nodded and reached for the phone.

"Yes, would you come to my office, please? I have two men who require an escort. Thank you." He hung up the phone and he met Gaucho's reproachful stare. "I'm sure we'll continue this conversation later."

"Of course. Thank you for your help, Mr. Wiley," Top said, obviously wanting to act as an intermediary before Gaucho launched himself over the station chief's desk.

A moment later there was a knock on the door. Wiley said, "Come in."

Gaucho turned to see who was at the door. Instead of the Gunnery Sergeant, he found himself facing three men clothed in business suits and holding MP5s.

"I'd like these two escorted down to the holding area," Wiley said. Before either man could protest, Wiley added, "Have them shackled, gagged, blindfolded, and prepped for the move to the interrogation facility."

"What the hell is this about?" Trent growled.

"Oh, don't play coy now. You know why I'm doing this. You're both wanted for the murder of Elliot Peabody."

CHAPTER TWENTY-ONE

They had time for a couple hours' catnap, not that anyone really slept soundly, except for Christian's grandfather. While Daniel slipped into a peaceful reverie, the grandfather fell into a contented slumber.

In fact, when Daniel awoke, the old man was still asleep. For a few minutes Daniel listened to the gunfire in the distance. It beckoned to him. Old memories percolated up through his subconscious, not in an undesirable attack, but as a reassuring reminder. He'd learned to disregard the draining power of evil, instead allowing it to serve as a warning that there always lurked impending danger. It reminded him to tread with caution, lest fate carry him and those he cared about down the wrong path.

Daniel sat quiet, in the empty apartment they had been taken to, pondering how best to escape their current predicament. He watched as Christian attempted to get comfortable lying on the concrete floor. Cal sat in a corner, napping with Liberty's head resting comfortably in his lap. He wondered what Cal might be dreaming about and wondered how much longer his friend would continue to serve in this capacity.

Daniel knew, with 100% certainty, these missions would forever be his life's pursuit because out here he felt whole. He enjoyed the perks Cal provided his operators, and he truly appreciated the fancy housing in Charlottesville. It was just that Daniel was cut out for the simple life. He was most content with focusing on people, and had no real need for gathering things. He felt most comfortable, and authentic, while he was out on the road. Especially when he was the only one awake, protecting his friends.

Every operation was a new adventure to Daniel. They provided him with opportunities to learn about new cultures and expand his already broad knowledge of the world and its people. He felt himself inexplicably drawn to both Christian and his grandfather, not necessarily because of anything they had either said or done. He admired the grandfather's way in which he took measured steps, as if he were taking an extra half second to ponder things, whereas the majority of people just plodded ahead, always in a hurry. Then there was the way he looked at Daniel. There was no judgment there, just a silent acceptance as if he was saying, "*You're one of us, aren't you?*" He had taken to calling the old man "grandfather," just like the grandson, and the man had seemed both pleased and honored.

There had been few times in Daniel's life when he'd encountered a person who seemed to understand the intricate weavings of the universe as he did. He'd accomplished this in a roundabout way. First, through service to his country followed by a period of time in which he found himself stumbling through life, and finally finding himself and where he fit in this vast world.

The last time he'd encountered "his kinfolk" was when he'd met the brothers of St. Longinus, the secretive order tasked with doing the Pope's bidding. They'd been a wonderful surprise. They were warriors as elite as any on earth and were blessed with an absolute faith in a higher power. This seemed to enhance their abilities and guide their steps. It kept them grounded and elevated all at once.

It wasn't that Daniel had envied those men, and he didn't envy the grandfather, but he strived to learn from such friends. Now that he thought about it, surely there were women with the same insight, who were a blessing to everyone they came across.

The grandfather stirred and opened his eyes as if he sensed that Daniel was thinking about him. He turned, looked at Daniel and gave him a small smile. Daniel smiled back, desiring to know what the man was thinking.

Now they were all beginning to stir. Liberty hopped up from the ground and shook herself off.

"Here, girl," Christian said.

Liberty trotted over and was happy to give Christian a few licks on the cheek. For all the boy's bravery, he was still just a kid, and Daniel prayed that no harm would befall him.

The grandfather said something to Christian, and the boy looked over at Daniel, confused. There was a quick banter between them before Christian said, "My grandfather wants you to go with him. He says Cal, Dr. Higgins and I should go to the camp west of the city, with Liberty, of course."

"Camp," Cal asked. "What camp?"

The grandfather rattled off a few sentences which Christian translated.

"He says the military has taken the prisoners there, and we might find some answers.

"What about them?" Cal asked regarding Daniel and the grandfather's plans.

"They're going to see his nephew, the president."

"That's a great idea and all, but I really think we should get to the embassy. Maybe they'll have a way for us to contact our friends."

"No," Daniel said. "I think we should do what he says."

The grandfather nodded in agreement.

"Are you sure about this?" Cal asked.

"I am. Now," Daniel said, rising from the floor, "why don't we get going while we still have the cover of dark?"

Daniel and the grandfather wound their way through the city after leaving everyone else at the apartment. The old man led the way. He looked like a marathoner in his prime, never slowing except to look around corners and to stop when patrols neared. No words were spoken. They climbed atop buildings and hid behind cars.

Daylight was coming, and Daniel sensed the gentleman's pace quicken. Daniel had expected to arrive at either a modest mansion or a presidential palace, so he was quite surprised to find themselves slowing as they approached a narrow street lined with modest homes.

Daniel felt completely exposed as they walked right down the middle of the street, but the grandfather strode with confidence, as if he owned the place. When they reached the end of the block, the old man tapped his chest and pointed to the end unit and said, "Home."

"I thought we were going to help your nephew," Daniel said.

The man repeated the gesture. "Home."

They entered the unlocked front door. The interior was simple and tastefully decorated, as if ample money had been put into the place to make it comfortable, but not so much to make it appear ostentatious. The grandfather locked the door behind him. He stood in the middle of the living room when he called out. Daniel heard shuffling from the back of the small house.

His weapon was ready, should the need arise, but the grandfather stood calmly, and Daniel wondered if maybe he had a servant or family hiding in the back.

The first man to step out glanced around, cradling an automatic weapon. His face was slick with sweat. He looked alarmed when he saw Daniel. The grandfather said something to put the man at ease. There was a brief exchange, and then the big man motioned for the two to follow him to the back of the dwelling.

When they reached the kitchen they were met by two more men. One wore a blood-soaked bandage over his forehead and right eye, and the other bodyguard held one arm in a sling. They both carried weapons and had cast off their suit coats and wore loosened neckties.

The man with the bandage on his head walked over to Daniel. He was missing one eye, but he leveled his one good eye at Daniel and asked, "Who are you?"

The grandfather said something to the man, but that one good eye never took his gaze from Daniel.

Who are these guys? Daniel thought. *Friends, local security?*

And then his question was answered when a gentleman in a blue suit limped into the room. He didn't even seem to notice Daniel, but moved over to the grandfather and gave him an embrace. Then the grandfather grasped the man's head. The two touched foreheads and the old man said something softly so only the wounded man could hear. Then they separated, and the man looked at Daniel.

"My uncle tells me that you are American and can be trusted. Do you know who I am?"

"You're President Farah," Daniel said.

The president nodded. "I would say welcome to my country, but this is a very sorry welcome. These men are my bodyguards, and as you can see, only Ali has come away relatively unscathed."

"What happened to your leg?"

"It turns out that I am not quite as limber as I used to be. I took a fall as we were running away. Ali had to carry me when we ran for the car. I am sorry, how rude of me, I didn't catch your name."

"Daniel, Mr. President. My name is Daniel Briggs."

"It is a pleasure to meet you Mr. Briggs, and if you are a friend of my uncle, I consider you good company. Now, may I ask what is it that you are doing in my country? You don't look like regular military, and I would assume that if you were Embassy staff, you would be there."

The grandfather turned to face Daniel and gave him a look as if to say, "You can tell him everything. Trust."

Now was no time to hold back. Daniel gave President Farah the highlights of their journey, starting from the emergency message sent by Vince and finishing with their meeting at Camp Lemonnier.

"Where is Christian?" the President asked. "I know he's a resourceful boy, but I would hate to see anything happen to him."

"He is with my employer, Mr. President, and I'm sure they'll be fine."

The president of Djibouti shifted from one leg to the other, wincing as he put weight on his injured knee.

"As providence would have it, I believe we are on a similar mission, Mr. Briggs. It just so happens that before I had to flee my own presidential quarters, I had a conversation with President Zimmer. Would you like to guess what we talked about?"

"Our missing friends," Daniel said.

"You are correct. My only regret was that before I could tell your president more our connection was severed. Would you like to know what I was about to tell President Zimmer when I was unceremoniously chased from my very home?"

Daniel nodded with fervor.

"I believe I know where your two men are being held."

Now we're getting somewhere, Daniel thought.

The grandfather turned around suddenly, his hands held out wide, his palms pointing to the ground as if he were expecting to fall. He murmured something to his nephew who turned to his bodyguards and barked some commands. They scattered to opposite points in the house while Daniel stand firm.

A rattle of gunfire sounded from the back of the house, and there was a scream of pain from one of the bodyguards, no doubt. There was more rifle fire, and now President Farah, the grandfather and Daniel were crouched down in a defensive position. Daniel was about to suggest that they find a way out when an explosion rocked the entire building. The next second, the only thing Daniel saw was the concrete roof caving downward and falling on top of their bodies.

CHAPTER TWENTY-TWO

Vince came to slowly, like his brain was wading through a field of molasses. He couldn't remember where he was or how he'd gotten there. The first word that came to his mind was *Karl*. Where was Karl?

His eyes blinked open and then shut just as fast. He could feel a presence now; someone was near him. But while his inherent scanner was working, his body wasn't, so he kept his eyes closed, patiently waiting for his body's sensations to return. And return they did; this time with a vengeance.

It started with tingling, first all along his torso, then spreading down his legs, up his shoulders and down his arms, until finally there was a stabbing pain at the end of each of his fingers and toes. It felt like someone was poking needles in the ends of his hands and feet, shoving them ever deeper until they hit bone.

But Vince still wouldn't move. He tried to focus on taking calm breaths in and out and imagined himself on the rifle range, preparing for a long shot. That seemed to do the trick, as if his body was the rifle, and his inhales of oxygen were dampening it down to perfect stillness.

"I know you're awake," came a voice he didn't recognize. "Open your eyes if you'd like."

There was a hint of an Asian accent there, but so slight that he couldn't determine the dialect.

Vince eased his eyelids open, allowing the dim light to pierce his raw senses. He blinked repeatedly until finally the room cleared. There was a man standing in the corner, sipping on a can of Coca Cola. Vince's mouth watered at the sight, but then he realized who the man was. He was the foreigner from the camp who had taken him and Karl after plunging needles into their necks.

"Where am I?" Vince asked, though his voice was just barely above a whisper. His throat felt raw and dry. He found himself glancing at the can of Coke in the man's hand. What he wouldn't give for one deep gulp.

"You're being held," the man said. "Don't worry. You've been treated well. Would you like to see?"

Vince tried to move his head, and that was when he realized his entire body was restrained. He carefully checked his limbs, pressing firmly against the canvas straps, but they wouldn't budge.

"Here, let me help you," the man said, grabbing something from a table and bringing it over. It was a mirror. He held it up so Vince could see himself.

They'd shaved him. Gone was the scraggly beard and long hair, replaced with a neat high and tight haircut and a perfect shave. He now looked like what he was - an army colonel.

"Your body is the same," the man said. "You've been scrubbed and cleaned, and you will fully recover from the effects of the narcotics. I must say, for a man of your age, you are in peak physical condition."

"Where is my friend?"

"Oh, he will be along shortly. They're just finishing up his

bath. I am sure you're hungry. Would you like something
to eat?"

"No."

"Something to drink? Maybe one of these?" The man held
up the can of Coke.

"No," Vince stated again.

"Very well. As you can see, you have an intravenous line,
and you have been given fluids and nutrients during your stay.
Feel free to hold out. It's of no concern to me."

Vince's eyes roamed around part of the room he could
actually see. At first he thought he was in some kind of
concrete building, maybe a bunker, but when he looked
closer, the walls still had the telltale vein of wood that had
been painted.

"So tell me, how difficult is your training? Is it like they
say, only the toughest and smartest can make it through as a
Delta operator?"

Vince didn't let his emotions show.

"Are you sure?" the Asian asked.

Vince did not answer.

"Come now, Colonel. I thought we'd have a little conversation before the fun begins. What do you say? One elite
warrior to another."

"What do you want to know?" Vince asked.

"I have always been curious. In my country it is said that
Americans would never be a match for my countrymen. I am
obviously not that naïve. So you could imagine my excitement
when I was told that I would have the opportunity to speak
with not one, but two, Special Operations Detachment Delta
operators. So please tell me, Colonel Vince Sweeney, did you
always know that you wanted to be a counterterrorism
specialist?"

Vince didn't like the fact that the man obviously knew
who he was. How the hell had that happened? But he couldn't

worry about that now. It was far better to keep the man engaged.

"When I was growing up I wanted to be a dentist," Vince said. "Have you ever seen the movie, *Rudolph the Red-Nosed Reindeer?*"

The Asian man shook his head.

"Well, you see, there's this little elf in there, right? Elves help get all the toys ready for Christmas for all the kids. Well, anyway, so this elf doesn't want to be an elf. He doesn't want to make toys. He wants to be a dentist. Wouldn't you know, I must have watched that movie a hundred times, and that made me want to become a dentist."

The Asian man was frowning now. "Your level of sarcasm will not help your situation, Colonel."

"Oh, come on. You can call me Vince. Hell, you've probably seen me naked." Vince grinned at the man's obvious discomfiture. "Oh, I get it. You liked it. You liked seeing me naked. Hmmm."

The man turned away and set his can of Coke on a table. "I will bring in your friend, Karl Schneider. And I suggest you convince one another to play by the same sheet of music."

"Oh, yippee," Vince said. "We get to play music? I like music, too. When I was a teenager I stopped wanting to be a dentist. I wanted to be a rock and roll star. Please, when do we get to play music?"

The man shook his head, as if dealing with a petulant child who would never learn wrong from right.

"Talk to your friend, Colonel Sweeney. How you behave in the coming hours will decide whether you will ever see your home again."

CHAPTER TWENTY-THREE

It was morning now, and Djibouti City was starting to stir. Cal didn't know what the secret was, but somehow its citizens knew it was safe to go about their lives. Cal asked Christian about it, and all the response he got was a shrug, as if carrying on with your day after a military coup was normal.

But it turned out to be the perfect cover. As the crowd swelled, walking out of stores with groceries, it was easy to melt in with the rest of the pack. So off went the remainder of their group: Cal, Christian, Dr. Higgins, and Liberty, of course. She was on a leash, and she didn't seem to like that fact. It was either that or get even more curious stares from onlookers. They were a mismatched group as it was, and the last thing Cal wanted was to attract further attention.

Dr. Higgins gave Christian a few dollars to pick up some food, and he returned five minutes later with an assortment of pastries that were devoured in short order.

"The owner said there may not be a curfew tonight," Christian said between bites.

"Did he say why?" Cal asked.

"One of the other customers seemed to think that it was all over — that whatever happened has been fixed. So that's good, right?"

"What would be good is if I could use my cell phone again," Cal said. "I still have no signal, and from the looks of things, everybody else is in the same boat."

It had taken Cal a couple of blocks to figure out what was different. Then he realized that nobody was talking on phones. Nobody was looking at their cell phone screens, playing video games or texting. It was like they had time traveled back to the early 90s. The technology tether had snapped for however long those in power decided that the people shouldn't have a voice.

The sun was just peeking out over the buildings, but it was already hot. Dr. Higgins was sweating like an ice cube on a hotplate, but he never complained, taking careful sips of water as they walked.

"Let's take a cab," Cal suggested.

"Do you think that's wise?" Higgins asked.

"Looks like plenty of other people are doing it," Cal answered.

And they were. Just ahead, a mom and her two children stepped into a cab. Cal could see the relief on Higgins's face, and he wondered if it had been advisable bringing him along. The good doctor was phenomenal in his chosen field, but he wasn't a field guy. There was nothing wrong with that — you either were or you weren't. On a normal day, Cal would rather have Dr. Higgins at his side over twenty other operators, but this wasn't a normal day. Higgins was one of his men — his responsibility. So while Christian hailed the cab, Cal said, "Hey doc, I've been thinking; why don't you take the cab back to the embassy and see if you can find Top and Gaucho?"

Dr. Higgins turned and leveled Cal with a glare that he had never seen before, at least not from Dr. Higgins.

"Calvin, that sounds like you're trying to get me out of the way. Have I already become a liability?"

"No, Doc, I— "

"Well, good. Then we'll go back to the embassy together, after this is done."

Cal could have ordered him to go, if he'd wanted, but he had to trust that Higgins knew his own limits. Now that he thought about it, Doc had worked in the field at one point, and without Daniel at his side, Cal realized he was more than happy to have the doctor's counsel.

So, the three men accompanied, by the ever faithful dog, hopped into a cab. Higgins didn't say a word. Cal watched him in the side mirror, relishing the cool air blasting out of the vents angled toward his face. Christian and the cab driver struck up a conversation in what Cal now understood was Somali. They chattered on as they drove through the winding streets.

Cal really couldn't believe how many people were out. It reminded him of that first sunny day after winter when you got to step outside to enjoy your newfound freedom. There were people gathered in groups chatting among themselves because no longer did they have the use of their phones. Cal didn't know whether to view this as a comfort or foreboding, like the calm prior to the storm. What would have dictated the easing of the military stranglehold? Maybe the international community had gotten involved? Cal would've given anything for a two-minute news report, although that was something he usually spurned.

"He says the camp's up ahead," Christian said.

"Yes, yes!" the driver said, excitedly, pointing up ahead.

"Can you stop here?" Cal asked.

"Yes, yes!" the driver said, pulling curbside. When they

had gotten out, and Christian was about to pay, Cal asked, "Will you see if he can stick around? We might need him again. I don't see any other cabs driving in this area."

The bargaining was quick, and after handing the driver an extra bill, the driver put the vehicle in park and waved to them happily, as if saying, "Have fun storming the castle!"

The camp was surrounded by chain-link fencing topped with spirals of concertina wire. There were still mounds of dirt where the posts had been set in the ground.

"Someone put this thing up in a hurry," Cal observed.

"The driver said it's been here two days," Christian offered.

Not bad for two days, Cal thought.

The place was roughly the size of a small community college campus. There was one large structure in the middle that looked like some kind of sewage treatment facility, but other than that, there were lines of four-man tents with the door flaps waving in the early morning breeze.

As they moved around, they caught sight of roving patrols, but they didn't pay the group outside the fence any attention. When they cut around the corner of the encampment, more temporary facilities came into view. These looked like wooden huts with sturdy gray walls. Air-conditioning units were chugging along, bleeding as much power as they could from the gas generators they were hooked up to.

Then they saw the first prisoners. There was a group of eight escorted by four soldiers. Five prisoners had the light complexions of Europeans; the other three looked to be from the local region. It struck Cal as odd that only one of the eight prisoners had his head downcast. The others actually looked like they were having a good time. A couple were even smiling and chatting away, like they were on a Sunday stroll with friends. The soldiers looked serious, but not too intimidating.

For Cal, it all had the feel of the movie *Red Dawn,* the original one from the 80s. In that one, when the Soviets and the Cubans invaded the U.S., they established encampments for American civilians. Inside, life went on under gunpoint. Cal couldn't shake the feeling that this was some kind of replica of that same scenario.

"What do you think, Doc?" Cal asked.

"They don't appear to be mistreated. Either they know they're getting out soon, or this place isn't quite what we thought," Higgins said.

As if the universe had reached down to slap the words right out of his mouth, Cal watched in amazement as three of the prisoners, in fact, the ones that had been chatting a moment earlier, turned on their captors, and tried to wrench the guns from their hands. Two succeeded, while the third struggled. The rest of the prisoners just stood there, open-mouthed, until the fourth soldier panicked and started firing.

One empty-handed prisoner went down as the soldier's rounds pounded into his stomach and walked up to his neck. The others dropped to the ground to avoid being shot, and then one of the newly-armed prisoners turned and shot the firing soldier. He fell back, finger still locked on the trigger, firing bullets into the air.

The whole episode took less than five seconds, but the gunfire awoke the sleepy camp. As Cal and his friends ran for cover, Cal watched over his shoulder as more armed soldiers ran from the line of tents, rushing to join the fight. The prisoners didn't have a chance. Cal wished he could help them, but it was too far away, and the force was overwhelming. They put up a good fight, and must have been trained military, maybe even some kind of Special Forces, because they fought to the last, even as more rounds pounded in.

Finally, a heavy machine gun mounted on top of a Humvee, rushed into the fray. The last man standing actually shot the man firing the machine gun in the head, and yelled something at the oncoming forces. Cal couldn't hear what it was, and then it seemed, as if on cue, the entire mass fired in unison, silencing the man forever.

Dr. Higgins was huffing and puffing next to him, but when Cal looked in his eyes, he saw only grim determination.

"We have to do something, Calvin."

Cal was about to ask Higgins how in the world he planned to do that, but Christian spoke up first.

"Cal, I have a plan. We should get back to the city before anyone sees us."

At that moment, Cal felt like he was rooted to that spot. For some reason – call it warrior instinct – he now knew, without the shadow of a doubt, that Vince and Karl were in that camp. *What I wouldn't pay for a platoon of rangers right now*, Cal thought, and then he turned to lead the way back to the city, but before he could take another step, he was greeted by a ghostlike face. His weapon rose to greet the apparition.

The ghost smiled at Cal. "Fingers straight and off the trigger unless you intend to shoot, Boss." It was Daniel's voice and now Cal recognized his friend. He was covered in what looked like gray dust from head-to-toe. He wasn't alone; Christian's grandfather was there, and he walked over to hug Christian. There was another man he didn't recognize, at least not at first.

"Cal, this is President Farah," Daniel said.

And that's when it clicked. What the hell was Daniel doing here with the president of Djibouti? The man was leaning heavily on a cane.

"Did you see what happened, Mr. President?" Cal asked, meaning the shootout at the prisoner encampment.

President Farah nodded. "I must do something about it. They think I'm dead, but thanks to your friend, I'm not."

The grandfather walked over and patted Daniel on the shoulder as if to say, *"See, I told you this one would come in handy."*

"I have an idea," Christian said.

Rather than look down at the boy, and treat him like a child, President Farah asked, "What is your idea, Christian?"

They all listened, and while Cal thought it was ludicrous, bordering on suicide, the rest of the men nodded, even Daniel.

"Very well," Farah said. "Let us see if we can put your plan into action."

The decision was made, and Cal felt like he was being swept away in a sandstorm of craziness.

CHAPTER TWENTY-FOUR

MSgt Trent was just nodding off when the door to the interrogation room burst open. It was one of the three CIA clowns who had brought them down to the sublevel. In the fluorescent-lit room, Top had lost all track of time, so he and Gaucho spent the hours glancing at each other occasionally, because they couldn't speak through the gags. Movement was impeded since they were shackled to chairs bolted to the floor.

The guy monitoring them didn't say a word, just walked up to Gaucho, grabbing him by the beard, and punched him in the sternum. Gaucho doubled over, the chains of his shackles clanging. As Gaucho let out a stifled moan, Top pulled against his restraints, and tried to say, *"Come and hit me,"* but the words never got past the gag.

"Ah, the big boy wants some too!" The guy stepped in front of Top, his once-serious face replaced with a smile. He eased out of his suit coat, folding it neatly and setting it aside. "How about you, big ape? You tell me where you want it."

Top stuck out his chin.

"Ooh, you're a tough guy. You know, you never should have messed with Wiley, because when you tangle with Wiley, you have to deal with me." He rolled up his shirtsleeves, and stretched his arms. "Now, let's see. A couple jabs to the nose, an uppercut to the chin, or maybe a roundhouse." He was bobbing left and right now, like a boxer preparing for a fight.

Why did idiots like him always think that talking made them more menacing? To Top, it just made him look like more of what he really was — a moron with a meathead mentality. One important thing separating MSgt Willy Trent from other men his size: he had learned to think first and speak later.

"Okay, jarhead, I'm not going to make this easy for you. I'll let you guess what's coming."

The first hit was a right blow that caught him across the cheek. Top had gauged the timing and the distance, and thus he had gone with it, snapping his head right to go with the swing. It stung, but he had suffered much worse. Then, just like he had forecast, a second later, the jab came from the opposite side. Again, he went with the move. He could see that the guy had tried to surprise him. However, Top had been involved in too many fights and trained countless fighters to be bamboozled by this man's mediocre talent.

Next came a quick one-two jab to the nose. There was really no avoiding that one, and tears sprang involuntarily into Top's eyes. Blood gushed from his nose a moment later.

"You're not looking so pretty now, huh, big man?" The punk took a couple more slaps at empty air. "Yeah, real tough guy!"

Top blinked away the tears, clearing his vision. Classic. The guy was setting up for some Kong Fu Karate finale, like he was planning to reenact Bruce Lee in *Enter the Dragon*. The guy planted his weight on his left foot, using his hips to pivot into the momentum of the punch, a vicious uppercut that had just as much of a chance of breaking the man's hand as possibly breaking a normal man's jaw.

But Top was no normal man, and he watched with adrenaline heightening his senses as the man's body came up, hips turning, feet, arms, and legs pressing skyward. Top had been leaning forward on purpose, and in one quick movement, he sat back, and whipped his head down. When the man's hand connected, it wasn't with Top's chin but instead with his forehead. Top felt the man's bones crunch, and wished he could have seen the defeated and surprised look in the man's eyes.

After the initial blow, Top didn't hesitate. Grabbing the chair with both hands, Top planted his feet and pushed up with all his might. The CIA man was falling back now, holding his crushed hand, completely unaware of what was unfolding in front of him. One pop became two, and two became four, and MSgt Trent, still shackled to the chair was no longer bolted to the floor but charging forward.

The man looked up just in time to see that same vicious forehead slam into his nose, and his eyes rolled back. Top's momentum was so great that the guy flew the remaining distance headfirst into the door he had entered a minute earlier. He hit the door with a sickening thump before flopping unconscious to the ground.

That was all well and good, but how the hell would they get out of the room? Sure, the Marine's titanic strength had released the chair from the bolts, but he had no idea how he would release the shackles.

There was a knock at the door. Top looked back at Gaucho, who pointed back to where Top's chair had been bolted with his eyes, as if to say, "*Get back there now!*" But the Marine had a better idea. Using the legs of the chair, he was somehow able to move the unconscious man's sandbag body out of the way, so the door could swing inward. Then Top took a position behind the door as well.

The knock repeated with still no reply. There was a jingle of keys and something was inserted in the lock, and the doorknob turned. MSgt Trent prepared to spring himself against the door, trapping the next target, but he happened to look right, and saw Gaucho shaking his head. He wasn't looking at whoever was in the doorway. He was looking at Top.

"Marsten?" a familiar voice sounded from the doorway.

Top backed away, and three Marines strolled in, weapons ready. They came in cautiously, and when Gunny Whitaker found Top, standing over the body of the CIA man, he actually laughed.

"At least you took care of Marsten," Gunny Whitaker declared, pointing to the body laid out on the floor. He took out a set of keys, and he unlocked Top's wrist and ankle cuffs. "You really look like crap, Top. Did Marsten do that?"

Top nodded as he untied the gag. The other Marines were taking care of Gaucho.

"Geez, Gunny, I was about to kick your ass, too!" Top said.

"Now, why would you want to do that? We're here to save you. You want me to fix that nose for you?"

Top touched his nose and winced.

"I don't know; I was thinking about keeping it. Maybe the ladies would like it."

"I guess if you know any women who like the Wicked Witch of the West look, sure. Seriously, let me take a look at that."

After a cursory examination, Whitaker declared, "Yeah, I can fix it."

"Maybe I should see a doctor for this," Top said, retreating a step.

"Of course I'm sure. My first platoon commander gave us a five-minute hip-pocket class for resetting noses."

Top gave him a wry look. "Are you serious?"

Gunny put his hands up and smiled. "All right, you got me. No more messing around. One of my best friends is a corpsman. He showed me how to do a lot of things, like inserting IVs, setting shoulders, and fixing noses like yours. Now, would you mind if I get down to business? We really need to get out of here."

Top nodded and took one step forward. Once Top's nose was almost as good as new, and they had shackled the CIA man to Gaucho's chair, Top asked "How did you know we were down here?"

"Top, I know it's been a long time since you've been a gunny, but when you held my current rank, didn't you have little birdies that told you exactly what was going on in your unit?"

"I did."

"Well, it's no different here. Between you and me, Wiley's a real prick."

"You're really sticking your neck out for us. How come?"

"Marines take care of Marines, right?"

"Come on, Gunny. It's gotta be more than that."

"You're right. I made a couple calls, and my friends told me that, if I had to make the choice between you and Mr. Wiley, I should choose you every time."

"I'd love to know who your friends are."

"Well, the first I could tell you, but then I'd have to kill you. The second—let's just say he wears a few stars on his collar and he lives at 8th and I streets."

"The commandant?" Gaucho asked. "How do you know him?"

"Well, I don't, really, I just called Headquarters Marine Corps to see if they could pull your file, and wouldn't you know it, instead of getting some junior officer on duty, the commandant himself picked up. When I asked him if I could talk to the duty officer, he said that was him. He sent the captain home because his wife was having a baby. Can you believe that?"

Top and Gaucho both nodded.

"We're well acquainted with General McMillan."

"So anyway, he asked me what I needed, and I told him that there was a former Marine in CIA custody here in Djibouti. You can imagine that he was pretty interested about that. Then he really blew me away. When I told him that I had made the acquaintance of MSgt William Trent, he knew exactly who I was talking about."

"He's a good man," Top said.

"The best," Gaucho added.

Gunny Whitaker nodded solemnly, as if the fact that the current commandant was a Marine's Marine was holy writ.

"Do you want to know what his exact words were? The commandant told me that if I were a staff noncommissioned officer worth my salt, I should do everything in my power to make sure the two of you were personally delivered to the airport."

"The airport?" Gaucho asked.

"He said something about a package arriving, and that you should be there when it did. I've got the Humvee waiting out back, so we should get out of here before Wiley's men figure out what's going on."

"What about the military roadblock out front?" Top asked.

"Shoot, I forgot you've been down here for a while. They all went home. Everything's returned to a state of normalcy, so it shouldn't take but ten or fifteen minutes to arrive at the airport."

"Well, hell! What are we waiting for?" Gaucho exclaimed. "Let's go!"

Top added, "I sure as heck hope that package turns out to be girls in hula skirts prepared to serve us whatever cocktails we would like. You know what, Gunny? I could sure use one or two right about now."

CHAPTER TWENTY-FIVE

A ir Force One touched down at Djibouti-Ambouli International Airport with the same tip-top precision that always amazed MSgt Trent. They'd arrived at the airport as promised and Gunny Whitaker had left them on the tarmac with a company of marines and a handful of Special Forces sent over from Camp Lemonnier. Everyone from the company commander on down had been tight-lipped about what the package hinted at was supposed to be, and so it had come as a complete surprise when Air Force One came into view.

"You think it's smart of him to be here?" Gaucho inquired.

"Come on, man. Whoever took over the Djibouti government might have been crazy, but they're not foolish enough to attempt to take a shot at our president. Do you know the kind of heat that we'd bring down on this place?"

And that was all that was said regarding the matter until they met the president at the bottom of the ramp. Zimmer was wearing an armored vest and combat boots. He was holding a helmet in his right hand which he switched to his left to greet Top and Gaucho.

"Welcome to Djibouti, Mr. President," Top said cheerily. Zimmer's eyes went wide when he saw Top's face. "Ah, it's nothing to worry about, Mr. President," Top assured him.

One of the Secret Service agents was giving Top a look like he appeared too scruffy and beat up to be seen in the presence of the president. Top ignored him.

"Have you heard from Cal?" Zimmer asked.

"Not a thing. Our phones still aren't working. Do you have any idea how they did that?"

"We've got some people working on communications," the president said. "They hope to have everything back up and running very soon. Now, I was told to request to speak with Captain Gray."

The Marine captain commanding a company escort stepped forward.

"I'm Captain Gray, Mr. President."

The president offered his hand and said, "The commandant says you're going to give us a ride over to Camp Lemonnier, is that correct?"

"Yes, sir. Bravo company's waiting just outside. I'll get them in here and get loaded up as soon as you give me the word."

The president looked at the head of his protective detail who nodded.

"All right then, Captain. Let's go."

The airport was adjacent to Camp Lemonnier. The CO of the base had obviously taken every precaution along the planned route. There were snipers on roofs and armored vehicles blocking every street that could empty in their path. Not only that, the convoy commander was treating the trip like a fly-by in Taliban country.

When they arrived at the command post they were greeted by a Marine general and a Navy captain.

"Mr. President, welcome to the Republic of Djibouti, and to our humble home here at Camp Lemonnier," the general said, saluting, followed a split second later by the captain.

"Thank you, General, and I hope you don't think I'm being rude when I ask, but I didn't know that Camp Lemonnier was a flag posting."

The general chuckled. "The president came prepared," he said to a smiling captain.

"Actually, sir, I pinned on my stars three days ago. Captain Chavez here is my replacement. What better time to conduct a turnover than when all hell is breaking loose? Now if I might suggest, gentlemen, let's step inside. The Djibouti sun hath no fury but for the white-skinned man." Everyone chuckled dutifully except for the Secret Service agents.

"Actually, General, I was wondering if you could do me a favor," Zimmer said.

"I am at your disposal, sir."

"How long do you think it would take to get all your troops assembled? Say, except for those on duty?"

"Well, Mr. President, this might just be your lucky day. Most of them are assembled over at the "Thunder Dome," rehearsing for the change of command ceremony."

"Would you allow me five minutes with them?" the president asked, as if he really required permission.

"Yes, sir, I think the troops would be more than happy to see you."

A few minutes later, Trent and Gaucho were standing at the back of what had been dubbed the Thunder Dome. It was an amphitheater of sorts and consisted of a covering that looked like somebody cut off the ends of a Quonset hut. Not exactly like the Mad Max movie set, but the land around it was reminiscent of the film's geography. The floor was a basketball court covered in folding chairs filled by the troops posted at Camp Lemonnier.

The general took the stage first and in a booming voice amplified by the microphone commanded, "Attention on deck."

The entire assemblage jumped to their feet and stood at attention as the president walked onto the stage.

"At ease. Please take your seats," President Zimmer said. The troops did as they were ordered, and Top could feel the tension in the crowd. They didn't know why their commander in chief was present. They were still in the midst of a crisis, and some of them probably thought the president was crazy for flying in at a time like this.

"What do you think he's going to say?" Gaucho whispered.

"I don't know. Just listen."

The president began, "First, I'd like to thank you men and women who have volunteered to serve so far from home. I respect your sacrifice and America honors you for it." There was a smattering of applause and then silence resumed. "I come to you with a confession. In the coming weeks, you're going to hear more from both sides of the aisle about why I've come, but I wanted you to hear it from me first. You are owed the truth, because if there's anything I've learned from you troops, it's that the truth comes first, politics be damned."

There was a raucous wave of stomps and cheers encouraging him to continue.

"I am your commander in chief and there are some who might argue that you, and subsequently your lives, are at my disposal. They've got it backwards. It should be the other way around. The bureaucrats walking the halls that George Washington, Thomas Jefferson and Abraham Lincoln once did, are truly the ones at *your* disposal. Those aren't just empty words.

This is something that I believe in wholeheartedly. It is a truth that has been stamped on my soul and burned into my heart."

"I come to you today to confess to you that I failed two of your brethren. I let them enter harm's way fully understanding the threat, but also thinking with a politician's mind that if they were discovered they could just as easily be disavowed, cast aside as if they didn't really matter. I tell you, I'm ashamed of myself. I'm ashamed that I, or anyone else, has ever taken the liberty of casting you to the wolves. So this is the real reason I'm here standing before you today. I am here to locate those men, and I give you my solemn promise that I will do anything and use each and every resource at my disposal to ensure these two brave men come home. But I can't do it alone. I stand before you, not as your president, but as a fellow American who would rather die than see his countrymen tortured or ransomed to the highest bidder. So I ask, who will help me? Who will stand with me to show the world that America is not a place where we differentiate between service, color or creed? We are all Americans, and we'll be damned if anyone messes with our brothers and sisters."

The gathered troops jumped to their feet in perfect unity, yelling and screaming their approval, raising their hands, calling out, "I'll come with you!", "Damn the torpedoes!" and "God bless America!"

———

The old man with the peg leg sticking out of his baggy trouser pants looked up briefly from his sweeping. He'd somehow figured out how to do his job even while on crutches. He leaned precariously as he swept pieces of dust and rocks into a dust pan that he held with his good foot.

The cheers were still echoing from the Thunder Dome, and he'd heard each word the American president had spoken.

He took his time cleaning his little path, and when he was done, he cast the debris into a trash can and made his way back to the storage shed that Camp Lemonnier's temporary workers utilized.

He set the broom in its rack and hung the dust pan on a nail on one of the structure's wooden posts. He sat down on a small wooden bench and rubbed his sore upper thigh. Then he reached behind the bench and uncovered a metal toolbox.

Its top shelf was filled with screwdrivers, loose nuts, bolts, and a rusted tape measure. He lifted out the tray and switched on the radio hidden underneath. In rapid Somali, he called in his report, waited for confirmation that the message had been received, and then he switched off the radio. He replaced the tray in the toolbox and rubbed his leg again.

His shift was over. It was now time to go home to see his wife, in time for lunch. She would be happy to hear about his day.

CHAPTER TWENTY-SIX

Cal had no idea how Christian and his grandfather had done it. The first trio was a man and his three sons. The man nodded to President Farah, and then took up a position behind him. Then an old woman hobbled up, touched President Farah's hand reverently and took a place in the line.

On and on it went. They came on foot, on bicycles, on motorcycles and in cabs.

The president's people: Rich, poor, old and young gathered and waited. More joined them, they also gathered and waited. Happy cries rose up when those who had heard the president was dead saw that the rumors had not been true. And President Farah was gracious with them all — shaking hands, giving hugs to others. Cal could see the swelling pride in the man who had almost been dead hours before.

"There's got to be thousands of them," Cal said to Daniel. "How do you think he did it?"

"I think it was the grandfather," Daniel said turning to the old man who watched it all calmly, with his knowing look.

"Do you really think this will work?"

Daniel just smiled. "I came along for the ride; I didn't care which way it went."

Even Liberty seemed to be enjoying the spectacle. Thousands of new smells, yet she stood resolute next to Cal, ready to move whenever she was told.

On and on they came, answering the call that spread like wildfire. And then suddenly, like he had known that their ranks had swelled to capacity, the grandfather walked up to his nephew and whispered something in his ear. Christian produced a bull horn and gave it to President Farah, who, with the help of some men from the crowd, climbed into the bed of a pickup truck. The crowd hushed. He spoke first in his native tongue and then switched over to English, translating as he went.

"I thank you all for coming today. As you can see, rumors of my death were greatly exaggerated. They tried, they really did," President Farah lifted up his leg to show the crowd. "But thanks to the assistance of family and some very good friends," he looked down at his uncle and then to Daniel and Cal, "I am still here. But now, we must deal with those who believe they can use our country and our peaceful people for their evil ways. But before we go, I ask that we not leave with anger on our lips or hate in our hearts, but with love for one another and love for the friends who we must help. If you have brought weapons, please leave them behind. Let us not give our misguided brothers and sisters an excuse to produce further bloodshed. Let us now go, brothers and sisters, and show the world that we are a strong and caring people, and we will not be intimidated or bested by madmen who seek to imprison us."

The crowd erupted in cheers that shook the windows and the buildings all around them. Cal helped President Farah down from the truck and asked, "Mr. President, are you sure you want to do this? It's really not safe."

Farah eased himself to the ground. "We must have faith. I have faith in my people. But I'm not a stupid man. I suggest that you and your friends ignore my request and bring your weapons, just in case." He threw Cal a wink, took a firmer hold of his cane and stepped off to lead his people.

———

They were able to mount one thousand military personnel from Camp Lemonnier out of the roughly four thousand stationed there. More wanted to go along, if only to watch their president lead the charge; but in the end it was decided that based on the number of vehicles they had readily available, and the sheer number that could actually move through the streets, a thousand would do.

A team of SEALs and a Platoon of Marine Raiders were fanned out in front, but not too far out in front. The president had been specific on that order. The lead element would get eyes on, but that was all, and so off they rumbled. The cavalry was on its way.

———

Their progress was slow and steady. Daniel could see that President Farah was in pain. Listing slightly to one side, most steps were punctuated with a wince on the man's features. But he kept going.

Daniel felt swept up in it all. His entire adult life he'd been surrounded by violence, and now here was this man, no —not man—men. President Farah, the grandfather, and even Christian, and their minds hadn't flown straight to violence as a means to an end.

Daniel wasn't ashamed to admit that if he'd been the one in charge, he would have attacked the camp and killed as needed. He wouldn't have given his actions a second thought. It was just the thing he had to do. He would never have lost a moment's sleep knowing that he had done the right thing.

But now he felt caught in the swell. It was like that feeling he had with the grandfather, only this time the surge of feelings grew stronger. There were no angry shouts or shaking fists. In fact, the crowd was singing now, and although Daniel couldn't understand the words, he somehow felt the meaning.

And so, the crowd moved on. President Farah was singing with them, the pain on his face gone. Daniel drank it in; he relished it like a great life-giving stream that would soon be gone and might never be seen again. He tucked the feeling away, and hoped it would not be the last time he would experience it.

———

"Eagle Six, this is Sheepdog."

Sheepdog was the SEAL team in lead. Eagle Six was the president.

"Go ahead, Sheepdog," the president said.

"Ah, sir, we've encountered an obstacle. How would you like us to proceed?"

"What kind of an obstacle?"

"Thousands of civilians, sir. They're taking up every inch of the streets. We tried to look for a way around and tried to push through, but, well, but they're going the same way we are."

The president looked over at Top and Gaucho, "What do you two think?"

"It doesn't sound like they're hostile," Top said, "so maybe—"

"Hey wait!" Gaucho interrupted, "You think Cal and Snake Eyes are in there?"

The president picked up the mic, "Sheepdog, can you get eyes on the lead element of that crowd?"

"Negative, Eagle Six. Crowd's just too big."

"See if you can make your way around. We will just keep pushing forward."

"Roger that."

"I don't know. It could be a rally or a protest. See if you can get the embassy on the phone," the president said to the Secret Service detail. "Maybe they know what's going on."

The call was quick and the Secret Service agent looked up at the president and shook his head.

"Would you like me to call the commander, Mr. President? They've got helos on standby should we need them."

The president thought about that for a moment and then said, "No let's—"and then there was a cacophony of buzzes, dings, beeps and rings. Everyone looked down at their pockets.

"It's the phones," Gaucho said, holding up his cell phone. "They're working again."

"Top, see if you can reach Cal. See if he knows what's going on," the president said.

Top dialed Cal's number, but it rang and rang, finally going to his voice mail. He tried Daniel, and Dr. Higgins. Same thing all around.

President Zimmer was about to pick up the radio to call the SEALs when everyone froze. They all heard the unmistakable staccato of machinegun fire up ahead.

———

They were fifty yards from the front gates of the prisoner

camp when some idiot behind a machine gun just inside the fence line decided to shoot straight up in the air as a warning to the approaching crowd. Cal hated it when people did that. Where did they learn to do that anyway? Didn't they know that rounds always had to land somewhere? *Stupid.*

After a brief pause, President Farah continued walking toward the gates. Cal and Daniel were two steps behind him with their hands ready to go to their weapons if needed. Hopefully that wouldn't be necessary. President Farah put the hand that wasn't clutching the cane in the air as he walked, and he waved to the soldiers to show them that he was not armed. Another volley of machine gunfire was shot straight in the air, and Cal imagined what would happen if the rounds fell onto the heads of the crowd behind him.

"We come in peace," President Farah yelled. "Do not shoot."

The soldiers were looking back and forth among each other, and Cal saw one of them pick up a radio handset and speak into it.

"We come in peace," Farah repeated. "I am President Farah."

Now there was palpable confusion.

"Our president is dead," one of the soldiers yelled back.

Farah was now only twenty yards from the soldiers.

"I am not dead. I stand before you. Now, please open the gates so that we can enter. Your commanders were mistaken. Please let us in. There is much I have to tell you."

Someone from behind the ranks pushed forward, grumbled something to the other soldiers. He then said out loud, for whomever could hear, "Open the gates. I urge you to open the gates for the president."

———

After a tense examination, the soldier in charge declared that the man who stood before them was indeed President Farah. The other soldiers offered up their weapons. Cal, Daniel and Dr. Higgins stood nearby. But the soldiers were no longer speaking in English, so neither understood what was being said until Christian translated.

"They're saying that many of the troops have left, and that they were going to let the prisoners go soon. Sounds more like they're saying that because the president's here. Wait." Christian listened now. "They're here," he said excitedly. "They say Vince and Karl are here."

President Farah joined them. "Come. Let us see if we can find your friends."

All the soldiers were watching wide-eyed now as the crowd entered the camp, filling it quickly. The captain led the way to the center of camp, into the semi-permanent structure they'd seen earlier in the day.

"In there, Mr. President," the man said in heavily accented English.

"And the general? Is he in there?" the president asked.

"I do not know, Mr. President. He comes and goes, and I have not seen him since this morning."

President Farah motioned for the soldier to open the door. There was an empty anteroom that Cal and Daniel entered first, making sure to clear the room of any threats inside. Liberty bolted between them and began scratching on the door at the far end of the room.

"Open it," Cal ordered the captain. Cal called Liberty back, who came back with reluctance and sat whining at his side.

The captain fumbled with his keys and was finally able to unlock the door. Liberty darted into the darkened room.

"Damn it," Cal cursed, sprinting in behind her with Daniel at his side.

Now their weapons were drawn, and wisely the captain moved out of the way. Daniel flipped on the light switch, and Cal's stomach sank. All they found were two examination chairs, empty except for a heavy splash of blood on one headrest.

CHAPTER TWENTY-SEVEN

By the time President Zimmer and the cavalry showed up, the camp mop up was complete. All supposed rogue soldiers had been rounded up and were being held until such time as they could be questioned, and the real traitors were weeded out. Cal didn't think there would be many because the guys they left behind seemed to be the real soldiers, whereas the ones who ran had probably been mercenaries.

President Farah accepted Zimmer's offer for assistance. The troops from Camp Lemonnier would leave a company of Marines behind to secure the area.

"The captain believes that your men have been taken to another location. This morning was the last time he saw them."

"Were they healthy or had they been harmed?" Zimmer asked.

"He says they were treated well, but one of them looked ill."

They were discussing their options when the president received three calls in rapid succession. The first, he said, was from the director of the CIA, who had derived intel from the NSA confirming that a small convoy had left the detention camp hours earlier.

"So we just missed them," Zimmer said. "But they couldn't have gotten far. At least, I hope not."

The second call was brief and was an update on another situation he'd been monitoring.

The third was the most unbelievable of all and was the general himself.

"He says his name is Hachi. Do you know him?" Zimmer asked Farah.

President Farah nodded gravely. "Yes, I know General Hachi, and I am sorry to say that he would have been one of the last persons that I would consider to be behind these unfortunate actions."

"Who is he?"

"He was a friend. We went to grade school together and played together as children, but when I went to Great Britain to attend the university, he went to France for military school. It wasn't until I was elected president that we saw each other again. He had changed. He had hardened, but his position in the army was modest at best. Now it would seem that he has changed much more than I first suspected," Farah paused, remembering something. "If I recall correctly, he was briefly relieved of command when it was suspected that he was supplying our weaponry to certain Ethiopian rebels. He was, of course, cleared of all charges, but now it seems likely that another hand has been played."

"But why would he go to such lengths to kill you?"

"I do not think that was his original intent," Farah explained. "They first warned me, and told me to resign as president. They said I would be allowed to seek asylum elsewhere, but I refused. It was only then that they used force to oust me from office. My men were killed, and if it were not for Mr. Briggs, they could have succeeded in killing me. What is it that Hachi wanted?"

"He says he wants to meet. He says he knows where my men are, and he's willing to help make an exchange."

"And where did he say he would like to meet?"

"He said he'd call again in an hour, and that we should make our way to the airport."

"Mr. President, I don't think you should listen to him," the Secret Service agent advised. "We should wait and see if our assets can track the general and—"

"No. I'm going, and this topic is no longer open for discussion."

There were incredulous looks all around. Cal was about to speak up, but Zimmer held up a hand.

"We'll talk on the way to the airport, okay?"

Cal nodded, but knew, from the determined look in Zimmer's eyes, that it didn't matter what he or anyone else said. The president had already set his path, and Cal had the nagging feeling that his friend's decisiveness could soon be his undoing.

By the time they got to the airport, it was decided that Presidents Zimmer and Farah would take the private jet that was being cleared and scrubbed top to bottom by the advance Secret Service detail already present. Aircraft from the USS Harry Truman would provide air cover, while drones from Camp Lemonnier would scour the countryside, and track the plane's every move. When Cal volunteered to go with them, Zimmer denied the request.

"Come on, Brandon. You need to let us go with you." Cal urged that his friend to let his team go along, but could see the president was eager to go.

"I've got the Secret Service guys. We'll be fine," Zimmer said.

"This is stupid. I'm telling you, let the pros deal with this one. We'll find this guy; we'll get Vince and Karl back. Then we'll pack up and go home. You do not need to do this."

Zimmer grinned. "Aren't you the one that's always encouraging politicians to put their money where their mouths are? Well, that's precisely what I'm doing. I sent those two on this mission, and I'm going to get them back. It's not like I'm leaving behind my security protection, and trust me—" His eyes twinkled, like he was thinking of some private joke that Cal wasn't privy to, but Cal wouldn't have thought that anything was very funny at the moment. "Everything is going to work out. I promise. You do what you do best, and I'll do my job. Deal?"

Cal nodded, although reluctantly. "You're still nuts, though. You know that, right?"

Zimmer punched him in the arm. "Looks like you guys are starting to rub off on me then."

———

The peg-legged man waved to the baggage handlers and scooted on to complete his job. There was a small private aircraft up ahead, and he saw men who were obviously some sort of security detail hovering around the plane. They stared him down for a moment and then their eyes moved on.

The cripple took a left turn and soon came to a metal shed. He stepped inside and nearly staggered; it seemed that the small space harnessed the day's heat and multiplied it tenfold. He latched the door behind him, and pulled the cell phone from his pocket. As he waited for the other person to answer, he rubbed his thigh, and he considered taking the fake peg leg off for a moment. Then he remembered the security men around the jet and reconsidered.

He put the phone to his ear and moved to the flimsy wall. That aluminum side sported a crude painting of the ocean which he took off its hanger. He revealed a small hole and peered through it. From his vantage point, he could see the sleek aircraft as well as observe the security detail looking toward the private terminal where a group of men walked toward the plane. He confirmed one target over the phone and was pleased to relay the name of the other man.

The men boarded, followed by half of the security detachment. The men around the plane moved aside and kept a vigilant watch of the perimeter. Once the side door was closed, the plane's engine's pitch changed and off it taxied.

They were on the move, the man said into the phone, after which he terminated the call. He'd done his homework. Now it was time to leave. There was much more to be done.

———

The shooter scratched his nose as he adjusted his eye behind the laser sight. The plane was in view and it was taking its time moving over to the main runway. As expected, all other traffic had been halted.

Then the plane did something strange. Instead of going straight, it turned right, heading straight for a far hangar. He was about to call in the discrepancy when he saw the reason for the diversion. Three heavy fuel trucks were making a direct line for the terminal. The plane had turned to give them the right-of-way. The shooter breathed a sigh of relief. His blood was pumping fast, and he took one quick look around him. He wasn't in or even near the airport. To be there would be stupid. But he still couldn't shake the feeling that he was being watched.

The plane looped around the hangar, obscuring his view for a good twenty to thirty seconds, he estimated, and then the airplane came out the other side. It continued taxiing but faster now. The shooter knew exactly in which direction the plane would go. He'd been watching aircraft take off and land all morning long. He knew the rhythm of the place and felt his heartbeat quicken. His shot was coming. He flicked off the safety and settled in to watch. He had been selected because he never missed a target.

———

Cal and his friends were standing in the main tower, watching the plane carrying Presidents Zimmer and Farah accompanied by their security details. Cal still thought it was a stupid idea. He'd had a conversation with Neil. Neil was positive it would only be a matter of time before he, or probably one of the American agencies, tracked down General Hachi.

"Why are they turning?" Cal said, looking up from his phone.

"The tanker trucks are coming that way," Daniel answered.

"You'd think they would have had that figured out before they departed," Cal said, annoyed. The Secret Service was supposed to have the entire airport staff under their thumb. To have three tankers divert the president's plane, and force them to take the long way around, was one more thing to irritate Cal. "We should be on that plane," Cal said for the umpteenth time.

As if Liberty shared Cal's exasperation, she growled as she watched out the window, her front paws propped up on the windowsill.

Cal's phone rang. He looked down and noticed the president was calling. He answered quickly.

"Are you having second thoughts?" Cal quizzed.

The president laughed. "No. I just wanted to remind you to hold down the fort while I'm gone, okay? This shouldn't take long. I promise."

"Who are you – my mother?"

"Just be careful, okay?"

"I will."

"And Cal?"

"Yeah?"

"Thanks for everything, okay? I mean it."

"Yeah, yeah. Just hurry back. I'm ready to go home, and I'm sure Vince and Karl are too."

"Copy that," the president agreed. "I'll talk to you soon."

The call ended, and Cal watched as the plane appeared behind the far hangar. Then it taxied to the end of the runway, picking up speed. It lifted up from the deck, leaving in its wake a stream of dust.

"I told you this was stupid, right?" Cal asked Daniel.

"He'll be fine, Cal. Just let him—" but the word stuck in Daniel's throat. His eyes went wide, and then so did Cal's. A collective gasp and hush followed as they watched a white-tailed missile as it caught up to the launching aircraft. Time seemed to stop. For the first time in a long time, Cal felt completely helpless. The ensuing explosion of the aircraft tore the plane and its passengers into a million pieces.

CHAPTER TWENTY-EIGHT

A man the world had never seen before stepped up to the podium. He was dressed in a crisp military uniform. As he adjusted the microphone, his medals clinked together. He spoke with a clipped accent. He was trying to be proper, but when he spoke the language, it sounded a little more forced than he would have liked.

"My name is General Hachi. Until moments ago, I was a commander in the army of the Republic of Djibouti. Unfortunately, I bring disturbing news. Earlier today, the president of the United States, President Brandon Zimmer, boarded a small private aircraft with a Secret Service detachment. He was flying to meet me so that I could assist him in brokering the release of two American hostages who had been kidnapped by what we then thought was a terrorist cell. Shortly after takeoff, a short-range surface-to-air missile collided with the president's aircraft. I am sad to report there were no survivors. While it was first thought the culprit terrorists were Islamic fanatics, we have since found the guilty party was none other than the president of Djibouti himself, President Farah. With the support of my fellow generals, I have taken over command of the country and our armed forces. Not only are our intelligence assets searching for President Farah, but we have been given the full support of the American Central Intelligence Agency and their assets in the region."

"This is a sad day for the United States of America as well as for the Republic of Djibouti. I have no doubt that in the coming days, we will find the men responsible, bring them to justice, and get past this sad chapter in history. My office will release information as it is known, but until then, know that the people of Djibouti are doing everything we can to find the criminals who perpetrated this horrible tragedy. Thank you."

The live feed clicked off, and the man behind the camera gave General Hachi a thumbs up. Only then did Hachi step away from the podium. He ushered everyone out of the room, except one man. Once the others had left, the general spoke to his guest.

"How did I do, Mr. Wiley?"

The CIA station chief had been brooding in the corner during the speech, and Hachi could tell he hadn't heard a word he had said.

"Mr. Wiley?"

They'd had a tense meeting before his speech, and Hachi wondered if he'd have to dispose of the man. It would be a shame, and it would be risky, but he'd already come this far. What was one CIA operative compared to the president of the United States?

"My people aren't going to like this," Wiley said, scratching his stubbly chin. "I've already got one man in the hospital, and my boss is breathing down my neck."

"So find more people," General Hachi said, walking to the small minibar one of his aides had set up before the news conference. He poured himself a stiff drink and after a moment's thought, he poured one for Wiley.

Wiley didn't even look up from his contemplation, but grabbed the glass and downed it. "We've got to be more careful," Wiley said. "This could really backfire. Are you sure there's no way that this can be traced back to you?"

General Hachi shook his head and tasted his drink. He preferred Johnny Walker Blue, but all his aide could find was some knockoff. He put the glass down.

"We've been careful. The shooter has already been dealt with, and before he took the shot, his spotter confirmed President Farah was also on the plane."

"What about the remains? Have any been recovered yet?"

"What remains?" General Hachi laughed. "That warhead took out the entire plane. I cannot say I understand how all the technology works, but it works remarkably well. It will be months before any of the bodies are identified."

"I wouldn't be too sure of that," Wiley said, walking to the minibar to pour himself another drink. "It won't be days, but hours, until my government is all over that crime scene."

"Do not worry, my friend. I have already planned for that. It will be as easy as spinning another tale."

"But what if they find Farah in the remains?"

"We will find someone else to blame it on."

"I wouldn't get too cocky about that, General. You've never been on the receiving end of the FBI, CIA, and every other agency with three letters that calls America home. Hell, I wouldn't be surprised if half of Europe jumps in to give a helping hand. A lot of people liked Zimmer."

"Did you?" General Hachi asked with a sly grin.

"That is irrelevant. I wish you had consulted me before you did this. You have no idea how much this complicates our plans."

Hachi waved away the CIA man's worries. "Do not forget

we still have the Chinese on our side. They've invested too much money and other resources to back away now."

"I wouldn't be too sure," Wiley said, downing his second drink. "Mark my words, General, we only have twenty-four hours to wrap this thing up tight, and if we don't, we're both going to be dead."

———

They were all in shock. How could they not be? The had just seen their friend obliterated before their eyes. Cal replayed Brandon's last words in his head.

"I should have stopped him," he said. "He was just so damn hardheaded, but I should have stopped him."

"It's not your fault," Daniel offered, his usually placid face smeared with grief.

One of the air traffic controllers was chatting loudly to one of his coworkers. "Come see this."

There was a small TV in the middle of the tower. The ensemble watched as General Hachi told the world how the events had unfolded.

"It had to be him," Gaucho accused.

They'd already driven out to look at the wreckage. The smoldering pieces had scattered for hundreds of yards. It would take an expert team to piece it all together, if they even could.

They'd gone back to the air traffic control tower, hearts heavy, with the simmering taste of revenge on their tongues. To make matters worse, when they tried to talk to the Secret Service agents remaining, not one would say a word.

When they tried to call back to the States, it was like a steel dome had been placed over Washington D.C. Calls weren't being transmitted. The nation's capital was on lock-down. Cal had no doubt that Vice President Southgate had already been whisked away to safety, and at this time, they were probably rustling up a Supreme Court Justice who would administer the Oath of Office.

Cal thought of Marge Haines, his old friend, and President Zimmer's chief of staff. What was she going through? He'd tried her number but could not get through.

"We need to do something," Trent said.

"Yeah," Cal muttered. "We need to find that guy, and we need to kill him," he said, pointing at the TV screen where they had watched General Hachi's address.

CHAPTER TWENTY-NINE

Vice Premier Wang Ling tapped an unlit cigarette on his desk as he waited for the connection to come through. He'd been given generous leeway from the president of People's Republic of China himself. He'd considered it a great honor that the president had given him a free hand. He had been a longtime supporter after all, and had put in his time in some of the worst and most time-consuming government positions. But now, as vice premier, he was as close to the top as he was going to get, and he knew that. So to say that his job, and probably his life, were clinging onto the cliff face was a drastic understatement.

Finally, a voice came on the line. "Ling, are you there?"

"General Hachi," Vice Premier Ling answered, his words coming out with all the speed of a stalking snake. He had to be careful with this Hachi. Ling had considered him a peasant-like pawn, but he'd proved himself impudent and ruthless. He could approach the man a few ways. He could be subtle and carefully pry information out of the general, or he could just come out swinging. Vice Premier Ling decided on something right down the middle. "That was an interesting show you put on earlier, General."

"It wasn't supposed to be a show, Ling. It was supposed to be a statement of fact."

Ling lit a cigarette and took a long pull, letting the smoke fill his lungs and then expelled it from his nose. "How have the Americans responded?" Ling asked. He was having a hard time getting any information from his American contacts.

"They have not," Hachi responded.

"They have not?"

"No, Ling. I have had time to think about it. I think it is only natural they are gathering what facts that are available, and in time they'll come up with their own conclusions."

"You do not seem concerned."

"I would be stupid not to be concerned," Hachi said, "but I am a careful man and I am not without my resources."

"How could you do this?" Ling snapped, his patience now boiling over. "Everything we have worked for, every promise that we made, is now invalid. They will figure it out. If you think they will not, you are an imbecile."

General Hachi laughed. "The Americans will believe what we tell them to believe. If they do not accept the story concerning President Farah, then the CIA man you met on your last visit is already creating multiple contingency plans. What you seem to be forgetting here, Ling, is that President Zimmer flew into an area known for its general instability. We will, of course, apologize profusely and do everything we can to help, but it was not our job to protect their president from some terrorist scum who decided to slither across our border. He came to our country without asking, thinking he could do what America always does, step on us, take from us, and give little back in return. The time for that has ended. Now I must ask you, Vice Premier Ling, is this not the goal we have been working toward? Is this not the partnership that you wished when you first contacted me?"

"You were supposed to frame the president, not kill him."

"Have you ever seen combat, Mr. Ling?"

"You know the answer to that."

"As a soldier, you live with uncertainty every day. You grasp opportunity when you can; I saw an opportunity and I took it."

"How can you be certain America is not preparing air strikes and an invasion as we speak?" Ling asked.

"Because Wiley would have told me. He said there has been no movement and that the politicians in Washington are whispering that President Zimmer flew to his death of his own volition. He took too many chances, and he turned into a renegade cowboy. They are saying that maybe he got his comeuppance. So you see, Ling, the twisted halls of Washington are already working for us. A few more leads planted, dead bodies found, and they will have their culprits."

Ling wanted to tell the general that he was insane, but he knew it wouldn't do any good. Hachi actually thought he was going to get away with the assassination of two presidents.

"General, I order you to release the prisoners and turn yourself in to the American authorities. Make up some excuse and explain that you were not behind the attack, but that you had received information President Farah had been planning the assassination. However, even with this knowledge, you were too slow to stop it. Maybe they will show you mercy, but maybe they will not."

"I will not let the prisoners go, and I will not turn myself in," Hachi said, haughtily.

"Then you will not receive any aid from us. We will go to the Americans and tell them that our people will aid in the investigation, and you can imagine where that will lead."

"If you do that, Mr. Ling, I will give them your head, and the head of the man you sent here."

Ling knew he had overstepped his bounds as soon as the words left his mouth. Now his chest tightened. The man he'd sent to deal with the general and to prepare the prisoners was Ling's own son.

"You will not get away with this, General. Somehow, I—"

Hachi cut him off. "You will sit there and continue to do what you have always done. The money will continue to flow, and your investments and loans will increase. Have I made myself clear?" There was no answer from Ling. "I will take your silence as acquiescence. And be careful to remember this, Mr. Ling, if you decide to turn on me, not only will I tell the Americans that the Chinese people are just as guilty, but I will also see to it that your son is hacked apart, limb from limb. I will ensure he watches moments before his death as his body parts are fed to my dogs."

CHAPTER THIRTY

L ike much of the world, Congressman McKnight sat
in absolute shock when he watched the statement
from General Hachi. Of course he was horrified on
whatever level was still considered human inside him, but
what really had him frozen to the spot was the consequences.
He, a United States congressman, being considered up for the
Republican nomination for the highest office in the land, had
been involved in the assassination of an American president.

He quickly scanned his memory for any mistakes he
might have made. McKnight wasn't aware of any; however, he
continued to scan conversations and actions that might have
compromised his aspirations. Before he knew it, his mind was
spinning, and he felt the outer edges of what could only be
described as a panic attack. He'd never had one before, and
the panic gripped him as lucidly as a jab to the stomach.

Then he heard it. It was soft at first, like the grumbling of
a truck outside. Then it got louder. *Laughter?* No, not laughter. It was more like a chuckle from some obese man who'd
smoked for sixty years. It was gravelly. But when he turned to
look around the room, it was empty, except for himself.

There was no one there. He put his palms to his ears, but still he heard the laughter. Like an electric shock, he suddenly knew the sound was coming from his father, the specter, back again to mock him.

"Go away", McKnight demanded as the grumbling chuckle got louder in his ears. Now it echoed, like he was in some tunnel he couldn't get out of. "Go away", he said a bit louder. Finally, he screamed, "GO AWAY!" and the laughter stopped.

A knock sounded at the door. *Wait. Was it a knock in the real world or in his head?* McKnight tried calming his breathing to settle his racing heart.

"Congressman?" came a voice from the other side. The voice was familiar. It was real; it had to be.

"What? Uh, yes—"

"Congressman, is everything okay?"

It was one of the staffers, he couldn't tell which. He was still frazzled.

"What? Yes, I'm fine. I was just—um—practicing."

The staffer went away.

After a few more panting breaths, McKnight's clarity returned. There was no use worrying about it. He knew the damage had been done, and he would have to distance himself. How could he have been so rash? It was stupid. Of course he wanted Zimmer out of the way, but not like this.

When he thought about it more, he realized maybe this was the right way. The only snag was that he had the chance of being implicated.

And then his ruthless alter-ego grasped at hope. It had been Zimmer's decision to fly overseas, not his. McKnight had already been planning on using Djibouti as a major talking point. Could this have worked out better?

As a failure of the Zimmer administration, this could be the icing on the cake. Maybe this was a way to inform the

American people that while it was important to be a strong president who believed in the welfare of their troops, making such a rash decision was not in the best interests of the many. It just got you killed, and a dead president could not serve his country.

Already the words of the upcoming speech were forming in his head. It had to be a solemn, thoughtful, and quite presidential address to the nation to soothe fears.

As that recipe cooked, he thought of the Chinese and wondered what part they'd had in the president's death. He couldn't believe that they would be that crazy, and then it hit him. It didn't matter if they were behind it or not. They'd been aware, just as McKnight had been, of the president's movements.

The plan all along had been to get President Zimmer to hang himself, while also riling the Chinese. Unbeknownst to anyone, McKnight would be beneficiary of that tattered relationship. General Hachi would be the bad guy, and the Chinese would need an alternative. He would be that alternative.

The trick had always been how to keep the Chinese at arm's length while still keeping up with the illusion that he was their pawn. At the same time, he also had to maintain his appearance of strength and an image of incorruptibility.

It was one thing to cajole a wealthy corporate CEO into persuading his people to give away millions of dollars to a campaign, and then, once in office, politely brush him off. It was quite another to dupe what might soon be the world's largest superpower.

Yes, this truly was a blessing in a disguise. He could blame the Chinese. He could implicate them and use a strong foreign policy stance against the communist state to resume where Zimmer had left off. *Yes, yes. It could work.*

It was a strong move - a bold move. A move that America

wanted. A move that America needed. Like the days after 9/11, the American people would demand action, and Congressmen Antonio McKnight would give it to them. In exchange for bold action, the American people would hand him the presidency.

He ignored the phone calls and emails for as long as he could. Everyone wanted a statement, and he had to be prepared. He had to do it right, but he couldn't wait too long. He needed to be the face that Americans saw in the coming weeks. Not the vice president, but him.

He jotted down some notes, talking points, and highlights that proved he believed in President Brandon Zimmer. McKnight scribbled down the nostalgic tidbits that people could hold onto in remembrance of their recently assassinated president. The longer he wrote, the more he admired his speech.

Yes. Maybe everything had turned out the way it should.

Then he moved on to his next speech he would give to the Chinese. He had to be careful and do it in such a way that they would not turn on him. Maybe he could open another back channel, assuring them even while he browbeat them in public.

No, that wouldn't work. It was a major move. Something that could set back US-China relations for decades, because the Chinese never forgot. That didn't matter. No, it didn't matter one bit anymore.

He was annoyed to hear another knock on the door. He almost yelled, "Go away!" He didn't want to lose his train of thought. His mind was churning along now, words flowing easily onto the paper.

"Congressman, you have a delivery."

A delivery?

"Give me ten minutes," McKnight requested.

The staffer boldly opened the door, and McKnight

whirled around ready to berate the impetuous intern. Instead his eyes locked on what the young man was holding.

"They said it was perishable, sir. It's heavy, too."

It was a large square box, roughly twelve inches on each side, wrapped in bright red wrapping paper with a large white bow on top.

"Why don't you give it to the staff? I'm busy," McKnight said.

"Sir, the deliveryman was very specific. He said you were the only one who was supposed to open it."

A twinge of panic gripped McKnight.

"Did the Secret Service check it out?"

"Yes, sir. All clear. Or— of course it was, or I wouldn't have brought it in here."

The young staffer was giving him a funny look now, like the candidate was being a bit too paranoid. In McKnight's mind, the kid was being stupid. A president had just been killed. What better time to clear the decks than to kill the presumptive Republican nominee? But if the Secret Service had cleared it, then it should be okay.

"Just put it on the table."

When the intern was gone, McKnight wrapped up his notes and reviewed them once before looking over at the bright red package. He decided to open it. Maybe there was food inside. He was suddenly famished. Ah, but he'd better not eat it. He should have his people try it first - just in case.

The wrapping came off easily, like it had been done at some high-end department store at Christmas, the kind of job that only takes two pieces of tape. McKnight still wondered how they did that. Underneath the wrapping was some kind of luxury cooler box. There was a card taped to the top that said, "To a long and fruitful relationship."

Cheesy. Probably a bunch of bananas inside.

McKnight looked for a latch and finally found it. It was

carefully concealed, and when he pressed the button, the smell of flowers – jasmine cascaded out. When he flipped the lid back, a small puff of cool vapor escaped into the air. He looked inside, and all he saw were bright white paper carnations.

He pressed down on them to see how far they went. There was something underneath. When he reached down past the fake bouquet, he felt what he thought was grass. No, not grass. Something—

He moved the flowers aside. There was something dark down there – a green or black object. When he finally removed the last of the flowers, his heart felt like it had stopped. There, looking up at him with glazed fish eyes and a horrific yellow mouth, was the head of his moneyman, Jim.

CHAPTER THIRTY-ONE

"Yes, I understand. It will be done."

The president of the People's Republic of China hung up the red phone and stared at the painting on the far wall. There was Chairman Mao, forever staring down at him. He wondered how the beloved chairman would have dealt with the current situation. Surely he would have rounded up anyone he could think of and impulsively executed them.

But times had changed, and China was just seeing the fruits of their hard-fought labor into the world of capitalism. Now this happened and it could derail the entire journey.

Sometimes it was better to make an example, and at others, the mere threat would be enough. He could not decide which, thinking that maybe they could continue on their path, push the obstructions aside, and keep walking. But no, that was his modern mind thinking. He had to think in the old way. The nation must be preserved. It was how Chairman Mao would have wanted it.

The president opened a drawer in his large desk, and pressed one in a row of buttons. He slid the drawer back in place and waited. Minutes later, there was a knock at the door.

"Come in," the president said.

Vice Premier Ling rushed into the room, head bowed.

"Ling, this business in Djibouti is over."

Ling had the audacity to look up from his shoes, but remembered his place a millisecond later, and his head dropped again in deference to the president.

"But there are hopes, if we only have patience. Another piece of the silk road will be—" Ling stuttered.

"No. I should not have listened to you. You let things get out of hand, and now I must step in to fix your mess."

"But if you will—"

"Quiet!" the president looked at his underling with barely concealed contempt. Then his face softened. "Your son, is he still in Djibouti?"

"Yes."

"Good. That is where he will stay. I want the location of the two prisoners, and I want the names of all of General Hachi's accomplices."

"But Mr. President, I do not understand. My son is ready to—"

"You are not listening, Ling. Know your place. You have failed me, but worse you have failed our people. Not that I owe you an explanation, but this thing with Hachi is done."

"But we will soon have everything we need! The election in America will go our way!" The man was truly grasping.

"Have you been in contact with the congressman?" the president asked.

"Yes."

"And what did he say?"

"We did not speak." Ling was shifting uncomfortably now.

"What did you do, Ling?"

Vice Premier Ling told him about Congressman

McKnight's moneyman, and the present that had been sent to the congressman's office. For the briefest moment, the president was pleased.

It had been both a ruthless yet effective move.

"Who else knows about your conversations with McKnight?" the president asked.

"The congressman, myself, and you, Mr. President. He does not know that you know, but I am sure he assumes."

"Good. Let us keep it that way."

He fished a pad of paper out of his desk and threw it at Ling. The bumbling fool fumbled with it, and it dropped to the floor. He was quick to pick it up.

"Find out where they have the prisoners. Write the location down along with the names of General Hachi's accomplices. You have five minutes. Bring that back to me, and your position *could* be spared."

Ling actually ran from the room, although the president wondered if the fat man would fall on his face as soon as he got outside. Three minutes later, Vice-Premier Ling was back, his face beet-red, sweat sticking his fingers to the paper that he handed over to the president.

The short trip had given the president more than enough time to make his decision, but Ling didn't have to know that. He had a very important phone call to make, one that worried him, but it was necessary all the same. Like a plunging needle of vaccine, it would inoculate the Chinese president for the time.

Two stout men stepped into the room.

"Take Vice Premier Ling to my private residence and keep him there. He is not to leave, and he is not to make any telephone calls. Is that understood?"

Both men nodded; they understood the orders. Each man grabbed one of Ling's arms. Resignation was stamped on Ling's facial features.

"Do not be so morose, Ling," the president soothed. "It will all be over soon. I promise."

Vice Premier Ling looked up with hope.

"I live to serve."

"That is good, Ling. Keep thinking that, and I will meet with you soon."

The once-important man was escorted from the room. Once the door had closed, the president picked up the receiver and asked the operator to reconnect his last call. When the person on the other end answered, the president said, "I have the information you require. And to clarify, we had no dealings with any of your people in Washington."

CHAPTER THIRTY-TWO

"I still find it very hard to believe, Mr. Wiley, that you knew nothing about this. Wasn't it just two short weeks ago that you told me that every credible threat in this country had been dismantled or marginalized?" the ambassador frowned at the CIA station chief, taking intermittent puffs from the Newport that only made an appearance during times of high stress. "I have the Secret Service, Department of Defense, FBI, CIA, NSA all over me. Hell, I'll probably have Sesame Street wanting to give me a rectal exam soon."

"Mr. Ambassador, it's only been a day. I promise things will calm down soon."

"Don't you tell me to calm down," the ambassador snapped, even though that wasn't what Wiley had said. He pitched his still-lit cigarette into the garbage pail. Wiley wondered if it would go up in flames, but it didn't. He would have loved an excuse to leave the man's office. They'd had a decent working relationship before the whole mess with the president, but now Wiley realized the ambassador was not cut out for this type of high stakes showdown. Luckily, Wiley was.

"This General Hachi, where did he come from? Nowhere in any of your reports did you mention this man," the ambassador asked.

"Actually, sir, you did hear about him in your post orientation. He is, or was, a forgettable character. A fairly low-level general who somehow convinced the rest of the military establishment to support him and allowed him to take emergency control of the government."

It wasn't a total lie. No, Hachi had had plenty of support from Wiley that included future favors and plenty of cash. The CIA man had been surprised at Hachi's maneuvering. He'd obviously had a long-running plan for the future. He just needed an excuse and President Zimmer had played right into his hand.

"If you and I make it out of this thing—"

"We will make it out of this, Mr. Ambassador. I promise you that."

The ambassador snorted, lit another Newport and put it to his lips.

"Don't be so sure, Wiley. Ambassadors and CIA station chiefs have been relieved for much less than standing by as the president of the United States was murdered on their watch. Now, get the hell out of here and get me some answers."

"Thank you for your time, sir."

Wiley left, grateful that he didn't have to listen to another thirty minutes of a man babbling on like he'd never been in a crisis. Sure, it had come as a complete surprise to Wiley too, but he wasn't pissing in his pants.

It did feel like a nuclear warhead had just gone off and every bit of hospitable earth was now marred by minefields.

If Wiley knew anything it was how to slip through an explosive-ridden landscape without being touched.

He believed himself to be a relic of the past, born again in an age that wouldn't allow him to reach his full potential. What he would have given to be in this position during the Cold War, to be on the front lines against the Russians. As a young operative he'd read the stories and the after action reports over and over again. Djibouti was supposed to be his stepping stone. Now if he wasn't careful it could be the end of his career, or worse, the end of his life. He didn't think the second option was very likely.

He had eyes and ears all over the country and he had friends back home. More than one key politician considered Wiley a valuable asset. If things ever went south, Wiley had his insurance policies in place.

He was so absorbed in his scheming that he almost didn't notice his secretary running down the hall. She had a hand to her chest and her face was crimson like she'd just run the Boston Marathon.

"Mr. Wiley. Mr. Wiley."

Wiley didn't answer but just gave her a give-it-to-me gesture. She knew his moods well enough to take her place beside him and keep walking.

"Mr. Wiley, you have a visitor."

"Who is it, Jeanine? I don't have time for this right now."

In the past twenty-four hours, he'd had all manner of visitors. The FBI had sent investigators. The CIA had sent their own team. And the Secret Service, well they were a real pain in the ass. He wondered which ones had decided to make a return visit or maybe they had sent someone new - another thorn in his side. He had to keep it together.

"Sir, it's someone from the White House. They say it's urgent."

"Tell them to talk to the ambassador. I don't have time right now."

"Sir, they asked to speak with you personally, and they won't leave until they see you."

Wiley huffed, "Fine. Where are they?"

"They're in your office, sir."

"In my office. You let them into my office? That is my personal space, Jeanine. I've told you before, no one steps into that office but me. No one."

"Sir, they were very persuasive. Trust me, you'll want to see them now."

Great. He could feel the pain of an impending headache. He'd have to pop a couple of Motrin just to make it through the day.

He was surprised that there weren't any guards standing outside his office door. Surely, a visitor from the White House would have brought their own security. Then again, they could be right inside. Wiley straightened his tie and walked in. His mouth almost dropped open when he saw who was sitting behind his desk with his size fourteen shoes propped on his clutter-free desktop.

"Well, well, well. I'm surprised you stuck around here, Wiley."

It took him a second to remember the man's name. Trent. Willy Trent. The man looked much more menacing now. The last time Wiley had seen him, he had seemed jovial. He didn't have time to ruminate on that fact before someone grabbed him by the scruff of his neck and shoved him into a chair.

"I was going to say to have a seat but it seems that my friend Gaucho took care of that for me."

The man with the funny beard slapped him on the back hard. When he moved toward the desk, Wiley saw a pistol in his left hand. The short Hispanic wagged his finger and said in a perfect Ricky Ricardo accent, "Wiley, you got some splaining to do."

Wiley had regained his composure. "You're not from the White House."

"How do you know I'm not from the White House?" Trent asked.

Wiley didn't have an answer for that. He wished he was armed. He'd been stupid enough to leave his gun in the office safe. It was what he usually did before a meeting with the ambassador rather than have the ambassador's security staff take his weapon.

"You're both still wanted for the murder of Elliot Peabody," Wiley said levelly. "One call and I'll have your—"

"Oh, you want to get right down to it now, don't you there, Wiley? Here I thought this was going to be a boring conversation where you ask for a lawyer and blah, blah, blah," Trent said. "I hope we can get all the answers we need within, say fifteen minutes."

"I'm not telling you anything. You're criminals. For all I know, you could be the ones behind the assassination of the president. I will have you arrested and then shot," Wiley said with a sneer.

"Is this your thing, Wiley? You like to get people shot? Tell me, have you ever had to shoot anyone?" Trent took his feet off the desk and stood fully to his near seven-foot height. "Because you don't look like someone who could shoot another man. Sure, you can order other people to. There's plenty of people like you around, never willing to do the dirty work themselves."

Trent was walking around the desk now. Wiley felt his body tense involuntarily.

"Here's the thing, Mr. Wiley. I don't mind doing the dirty work. In fact, in some cases, I rather enjoy it. Twenty-three hours a day, I'm a law abiding Christian. That twenty-fourth hour—whoo-ee! I save that hour for assholes like you." A massive black finger that felt like a steel rod poked Wiley in the chest twice. "I'm going to give you one chance Wiley. You tell me all about your relationship with this General Hachi and how you put your pinheads together and decided it was time to kill the American president. "

"I didn't have anything to do with—"

Trent's foot kicked out like a mule, sending Wiley skittering across the room. He gasped for air that wouldn't come to his blasted lungs.

"You take a second to get your breath back, Mr. Wiley. I am not a cruel man, and I do not like to see my fellow man suffer. Do not take that as weakness. Just because I'm good with kids and I like puppies, it does not mean that I will not crush a skull with my two hands."

Wiley believed every word. As he struggled to regain his breath, the headache throbbing now, he tried to grab hold of anything, any idea that could get him out of this.

"It was Hachi," he was somehow able to say. "It was his idea, not mine."

"That's a good start. Thank you for your cooperation."

Trent reached down and pulled Wiley up by the front of his shirt as effortlessly as a child picks a stick up off the ground. He even brushed off Wiley's back like the kick had been some kind of mistake.

"We'll get to the details in a minute, but let's talk about Peabody. Why did you have him killed?"

Wiley was about to offer up an excuse, buy himself some time, but then the door opened behind him, and he turned just enough to see a hunched old man with a peg leg walk into the room. An old woman, probably the man's wife, followed him in and tugged the door closed.

"I'm sorry, sir, but you shouldn't be in here," Trent said politely.

The old man looked up. Trent inhaled in shock. "Well, I'll be."

The old man took off the fake peg leg, and put his real foot on the ground stretching his thigh, rubbing it to ease the pain.

"Peabody," Wiley said, relieved, thinking that his savior had come. "You're not dead."

Peabody ignored him, walked over to the trashcan, and spit a mouthful of phlegm into it.

"That stuff Sheila gave me sure does give me heartburn," Peabody said looking at Gaucho who ran over to hug the operative.

Wiley used the distraction and got up. He headed for the door planning to push past the old woman. A fist snapped out from underneath the old lady's robes and took him in the cheek, spinning him halfway around.

"What have I told you, Sheila?" Peabody was saying.

The woman was shaking her hand painfully. "I know. Not in the face. Damn that hurts."

The woman took off the heavy grey wig. Wiley didn't know who the woman was.

Gaucho pointed and said," Hey, it's the nurse lady from the hotel. You're the one that's married to—"

"Yours truly, my friend," Peabody finished for him.

"I thought—"

"Sheila and I met at The Farm." The Farm was the CIA's training facility in Maryland. Peabody went over to his wife and planted a kiss on her lips. "It was love at first sight."

"You need a shower; you know that?" Sheila said, slapping him playfully. Peabody grinned.

"But, you were dead." Trent said. "They killed you. You didn't have a heartbeat."

Peabody pointed at his wife. "Sheila was a CRNA, a Certified Registered Nurse Anesthetist before she joined the

Agency. A "gas passer," even though she doesn't like me calling her that. Not only do we make a good team, but we also bring a few tricks to the game. Sure, it meant that for a couple days it felt like the worst hangover I've ever had, and it was hell getting that goat blood off me, but it worked didn't it? I tricked you."

Wiley was listening to it all from the ground, putting it together, still thinking he had a way out. If he could only get to his safe. But who was this Sheila? Why had the CIA sent her here?

She must have sensed his concern, because she stepped over to him and stomped down on his back. "You're not as smart as you think, Wiley. The Agency's been onto you for years. They sent me and my husband here to keep an eye on you. Turns out that our timing was perfect."

"Peabody, one day you're gonna have to tell me how you convinced a woman who is not only smart but also beautiful to marry a guy as ugly as you," Gaucho said.

"Aw shucks, you're gonna make me blush," Sheila said, batting her eyes as she grinded the heel of her boot deeper into Wiley's back.

"While I'd love to hear the Army's rendition of *Kumbaya*, may I suggest that we take Mr. Wiley to a more secure location?"

The boot lifted and Sheila backed away. Wiley got up from the ground as indignantly as he could muster. His legs were shaking. It wasn't his first time under the gun, but his back, cheek and head were killing him.

"Look, seeing that Elliot's not dead, why can't we make a deal? Anything you want."

Trent's bear claw of a hand grabbed Wiley's throat and picked him straight up in the air.

"You don't seem to get it, Wiley. We don't make deals with pieces of trash like you. Gaucho, go get Doc."

What must have been a few seconds later, but felt like an eternity while Wiley was being asphyxiated, a chubby man in a checkered sport coat entered the room. He stepped up to where the enormous black man was holding Wiley in midair.

"So this is the infamous Mr. Wiley."

"Wiley, this is Doc Higgins and he's here to have a little talk with you. Don't try to resist. Nobody resists Doc Higgins."

From the confident look on the doctor's face, all shred of hope slipped from Wiley's mind. And somewhere between darkness and light, he remembered there'd been an infamous interrogator at the CIA by the name of Higgins. If this was that doctor, he realized he was done for just as he faded into unconsciousness.

CHAPTER THIRTY-THREE

"Yes," the guard thought, closing his eyes and raising his face up to the heavens. The heat felt like a blessing. He had grown up in poverty. His parents sent him away at a young age so they could die with dignity. He'd scraped by for years, leaving school before he really had a chance to learn of the world. Then, he had fallen in with a group of peers and found a new business: Security. Hassan had taken to it like a bird to the air.

Yes, there had been exciting times, but he found these long hours of guard duty most pleasurable. He had never admitted to a soul that he liked that time, but he volunteered whenever he thought it was proper. And so, after the brief insurrection when Hassan had been posted at the prisoner camp (he tried to forget about that unfortunate business with the Europeans), they had moved him to a new job. He didn't mind. He had a roof over his head, food in his stomach and while he wasn't a particularly violent man, he had no problem raising a weapon and fighting for his chosen employer.

This employer, well, this was the one to have. Who knew how long General Hachi would be the president of Djibouti?

The job was important. Hassan considered it a medal upon his chest, and even though mercenaries like himself never wore medals, he still imagined it.

When he opened his eyes, he was surprised to see a beautiful chocolate-colored dog with speckled white legs trotting toward him. Hassan was used to wild dogs, usually they moved in small groups, but this dog just didn't look like it belonged in that category. It was too beautiful, unmarred by the desert winds and blazing heat. To add to his surprise, it walked straight toward him.

Hassan wasn't afraid of animals, but he was still on duty, so he leveled his weapon at the dog. It cocked its head, as if curious as to why he had pointed a gun at it, then sat down on its haunches and stared at him. That curious look, as if the dog was asking, *"Why are you standing there with a gun pointed at me?"* The dog was not a threat, so Hassan lowered his weapon, patted his leg, and made kissing sounds to see if the dog would come closer.

It didn't. It just sat there, with the same look, tail wagging slowly back and forth.

"Lassie, Lassie, where are you?" came a voice, speaking English, from around the bend, the caller unseen. While Hassan understood English, he didn't speak it well, but he'd seen plenty of Americans, British, and Europeans walking past the ocean-side mansion since coming on duty. It was one of the ritziest neighborhoods in Djibouti, and was reserved for wealthy visitors and patrons. The neighborhood itself had its own gated entrances and private security. Hassan and his comrades were the second level of defense for the general.

"Lassie, here girl!" A form came into view, a light-skinned man jogging along at an easy lope. Hassan waved to the man and pointed at the dog. The jogger smiled and waved back.

"There you are, Lassie!" he said. The man picked up his pace, both hands raised in excitement, a leash in his left hand.

"Lassie, you really scared me, you know that?" The stranger was so focused on the dog that Hassan, by nature, did the same. He also looked down at the runaway, who still sat with her head cocked, looking straight at him. Then, to Hassan's surprise, the dog barked once, and the guard's hand involuntarily tightened on his weapon.

"No, Lassie, don't bark," the dog's owner said. When Hassan looked up again, he squinted. There was a glint of something between himself and the man, spinning, and that's when the flying blade caught him directly in the eye, plunging into his brain and silencing him forever.

———

The two guards had been mid-conversation inside the compound gate, but they saw Hassan go down. They couldn't tell whether he had just kneeled or fallen. It was their job to make sure nothing was amiss, so they went to their assigned duties like men on the eleventh hour of a twelve-hour shift.

One man went forward, easing the heavy gate door open, wishing that it was mechanized like so many of the other homes along the road. The second man stayed back, just in case. When the gate was finally open, the first guard on the scene saw that Hassan was on the ground and there was a stranger leaning over him.

"He just passed out or something! I think it might be the heat." There was a dog, too, a beautiful dog.

How strange, the guard thought, his eyes flickering back to Hassan.

"I can help you carry him inside if you want," the American offered.

"Hassan," the guard said, nudging him with his boot. No movement came from his friend. "Hassan," he said again. Still nothing.

"He doesn't look so good," the American said, reaching to feel Hassan's neck. Hassan was turned away from the guard, so he couldn't see Hassan's features. It wasn't until he stepped closer to the unconscious man that he sensed something was wrong. There was a wetness on the ground—Water or—And that's when he saw the crimson color of death running down Hassan's face.

Before he knew it, the Good Samaritan sprang up, leading with his hand, too fast for the guard to react. He suddenly felt a pain deep in his throat. He had been stung. He tried to yell out, with no voice. The pain went deeper, and then there was only blackness.

———

Cal held the man's body up while a volley of rounds came from the third guard, striking the second guard in the back. Then he heard the snap of rounds behind him, and sensed the body thump up ahead. Guard number three was down.

"It took you long enough," Cal said, dropping guard number two to the ground, who thankfully was wearing body armor. His friend Daniel trotted up behind him, Liberty coming in close too.

"I didn't want to make it too easy for you," Daniel said. "He knows we're coming now. He's heard the gunshots."

The rest of the neighborhood was secure. Djibouti commandos vetted by President Farah had seen to that. So here they were, about to visit the man who'd changed the world.

Cal and Daniel scanned the area as Liberty sniffed the air. The only person inside was General Hachi. The Marines had no doubt that he would put up a fight. Oh, how Cal wished, no he hoped, that Hachi would put up a fight.

General Hachi had, in fact, been in the shower when he heard the gunfire. He slipped out, tying a towel around his waist, grabbing his favorite pistol from the sink. He made it halfway to the bed, where he had a heavier arsenal stashed underneath. A growling form stalked into the room.

It was a dog. Why was there a dog in the house? At first, he thought that maybe his stupid guards had been firing at the animal. It had to be a stray. Wild. The standing hairs on the back of its neck rippled. He hated animals, ever since that night so long ago when he had been attacked outside of his home. Feral dogs, they called them, but in General Hachi's mind, vermin was a more accurate term. The attack had left him bedridden for over a year. He'd received a hundred stitches, and his leg never fully recovered.

His people had dogs, and that was what he had alluded to with Vice Premier Ling, but he never ventured near the animal's compound. Just the sight of the place made him want to run and hide.

The dog was barking at him now. Hachi's weapon came up, and a millisecond from shooting, the trigger already heavy on his finger, a suppressed gunshot rang out. It shattered the weapon in his hand. Casting it aside, Hachi fell back, grabbing his bleeding hand. Two white men stalked into the room, their weapons trained on him. One reached down to touch the dog, while the other moved to restrain him.

It wasn't that Hachi was surprised. Far from it. The last twenty-four hours had been nothing like he'd planned. He had watched in glee as the Americans turned on themselves and leveled their ire on the dead president. Then they'd turned to him and offered their aide and assistance. He met with FBI officials, the CIA, and a shadowy group of characters he could only assume were Special Forces who'd summoned him as the president of Djibouti. He had been glad, not only because they had come to the throne, but also because it legitimized what he had claimed.

Then, in the most peculiar twist, a man he hardly knew about, and only then did he know because of the election in America, the man who was to challenge President Zimmer, a man named McKnight took to the airwaves and attacked General Hachi. He had the nerve to tell the world that Hachi had been behind it all, even while other members of McKnight's own government courted Hachi's favor. On and on he had railed. It seemed as though on every station to which General Hachi tuned, there was McKnight's face, lashing out at him, demanding that the international community do something about this madman.

He was no madman; he was the future. He had been in control, and his country had cast aside the jackals of America, and forged a new partnership with a rising superpower. Unlike his predecessor, Hachi held no illusions that Djibouti would stand on the world stage with the likes of America, Russia, and China. But he had bet his life and career on the fact that China would prevail. When he made the call to Vice Premier Ling, he hoped that the man would help. But there was no answer; there was only silence. His once strongest ally had closed the door.

Yet, General Hachi would not give up hope. There was no proof that he had killed the American president, and wasn't it proof that the world wanted? Gone were the days of indiscriminate revenge, at least in the civilized world. The civilized world had cast such perverse actions aside, all for the sake of being modern and civilized. They were back to gentlemen agreeing to only shoot at each other in the light of day, standing across from each other, like the duels from the old days.

Hachi had believed, even if this McKnight and his

cohorts pressed their claim, that with friends like Wiley, he could survive. After all, wasn't it proper for deposed dictators to be allowed to go into exile? That had been his plan if he was to be ousted.

Now, here were these two men and their dog, bursting into his house—his domain! The nerve!

"Do you know who I am?" Hachi asked. The man with brown hair cocked his head and grinned.

"Why don't you tell us who you are?"

"I am General Hachi, president of—"

The shots caught him in the chest, two in rapid succession. He looked down and saw the pock marks, and then blood flowed freely from his torso and dripped down to his white towel. *This was not how it was supposed to be!*

He looked up at the men, and opened his mouth to speak, to demand that they get him medical assistance, but no words came. His chest seized. His eyes fell down to the dog, who was sitting now, looking at him curiously, with a silent question in those brown eyes, as if to say, "*Will you just fall down already?*"

But Hachi was a proud man. He had been cast aside his whole life, first by his good friend Farah, who'd gone off to university. He had been left behind, and it was only through begging and pleading with school officials that he'd been sent to the military academy in France. He'd worked hard and earned his place. Then he had maneuvered through the ranks, and indisputably been given the worst of assignments, but he took it stoically. He had always blamed it on Farah—always Farah. How could he have done it any differently? The world was what it was. He was who he was supposed to be, was he not?

Now, as he looked down at the inquisitive dog, he wondered what his life might have been like if he had taken another path so long ago. *If only he had thrown hate aside, lived a simple life, and married a beautiful*—

The thought disappeared into eternity, as the next bullets entered his brain, and the man who had been president of Djibouti for almost two days collapsed on the floor, dead.

The man with the blond hair walked over and checked for a pulse.

"He's gone," he said.

"Let's go," said his companion. "Liberty, come."

The dog turned around, and went to her master. He reached down, rumpled the fur on her head and gave her a firm pat: "Good girl."

CHAPTER THIRTY-FOUR

I t had been a while since Vince stopped keeping track of how many times he got hit. His only focus now was to remain conscious to ensure he received the beatings in order to spare Karl. He was not even sure if Karl was alive anymore. The last time Vince had been able to lift his head and look to the left, he had thought he detected Karl breathing, yet he couldn't be sure.

Damn you, Karl, Vince thought.

His friend had successfully goaded their abuser by using every racial slur ever invented denigrating the Asian culture. Now he was either dead or just a bloody pulp because of his actions.

"Hit me," Vince said through broken lips. It began again. The initial incarceration had rivaled a spa visit, but then, like a flip of a switch, it had turned dark.

He'd been trained to absorb all manner of pain, to put it all aside and keep his focus. But something inside broke when the Asian man informed them that President Zimmer was dead. There'd been genuine shock on their captor's face as well. For a time, he'd just sat in the room, staring at his hands.

It could have been minutes. It could have been hours in the subterranean room where they now sat. It was impossible for Vincent to keep track of time, but it had all changed with a single phone call.

The man had left the room and when he returned, his once blank face was now twisted with a hangman's cruel sneer. Vince knew it was all over when the man finally introduced himself as Major Ling.

He began the renewed conversation by saying, "When I was a child, five, maybe six years old, my father enrolled me in a martial arts school. I was young but large for my age. The first day a smaller boy sent me home with a black eye. My father gave me another. That night I went outside to where the peasant workers were doing some construction. I found a long two by four and propped it against the wall. Repeatedly, I hit that board until my hands bled. I did that for days. A week later, I returned to the martial arts school and beat the child who'd beaten me. I vowed then I would never lose again. I have always kept a two by four as a reminder of what weakness can lead to, of what defeat lurks just beyond the horizon if we allow it entry into our lives."

He'd shown Karl and Vince his knuckles. They were flat. He made a fist, but it looked more like a mallet than a human hand. Vince hadn't noticed it before, but he knew what it meant. After taking off his shirt and revealing his impressive physique, Major Ling slammed his fist into the metal door. He left an impressive dent for his effort. Then he held up his fist again. There was no pride there, just a silent, "*See, it doesn't even hurt.*"

Vincent expected questions to come; he always had. Interrogation was inevitable. Even after the initial flurry of punches, he'd steeled himself for interrogation, but none came.

Karl must have figured it out first, because that's when he

had started goading Ling. He spat blood at the man, hit him in the face, but there had been no bloodlust in Ling's eyes. He just waded in and levied the pain. Surgically, like he knew every pain point in the men's legs, arms, and torsos, but he saved their faces for his most crushing blows.

Vincent only lost consciousness once. He came to sometime later after Ling splashed a plastic cup full of Coca Cola into his face. The carbonated beverage stung as it penetrated every cut, jolting him back to awareness. On and on Ling went. Sometimes he would sit and take a sip of a freshly opened can that he grabbed from a bucket of ice near the door. Sometimes he would just stand and watch Vince. The Delta colonel was clueless as to his reason.

At one point, Vince had just asked the man straight up, "Why don't you just kill us?" Not that he wanted to die but that there seemed to be no reason for Ling's prolonged beatings of him and Karl. The only answer he'd received was a quiet, "It no longer matters."

While that might have given Vincent some measure of hope, he was no fool. A human body could only take so much. Already his breaths were coming with labored effort. For sure there were more than a couple of ribs broken, and if his ribs punctured his lungs, which he had no doubt they could, it was game over and lights out for Vince.

It was highly unlikely that Ling would lift a finger to save his or Karl's lives. There was a look of inevitability about the man now, like he was somehow accepting his fate even though Vince didn't know what fate held in store for his captor.

So he took the beatings with stoicism. When they slowed, he sensed Ling shifting to his friend. That was when Vince would lift his head and murmur something through swollen lips, and Ling would return to start the beatings anew.

So this is how it ends, Vince thought, *I'll die as a human punching bag*.

He always assumed that it would be a sniper's bullet or a miscast grenade that would take his life. He was very good at what he did. He loved what he did and lived with no regrets. The only regret wavering at the edge of his consciousness was that he hadn't been able to save Karl. But as Ling moved in for yet another one-way showdown, Vince focused on the image of the little red-roofed cabin atop some faraway hill.

———

Vince thought he must be hearing things now. He figured it was probably his ears going out, like one set of senses finally giving way with a pop, pop, pop. His eardrums must've been destroyed.

With incredible effort, his eyes eased open. That's when he realized none of the blows had fallen above his nose. He could still see. Maybe that's what Ling had wanted, for Vince and Karl to see every punch coming.

Devious, Vince thought in silent admiration. Even though the guy didn't have the balls to fight him man-to-man, he still had to admire the approach, like a boxer respecting the way an opponent threw a punch.

When he looked up, Vince fully expected to see Major Ling coming at him again, but Major Ling was gone. There was just an open door, and he could just make out shadows. Vince blinked, trying to clear his vision. There was a man with a dark mask heading in his direction. Two more men were following closely, weapons scanning the room.

There was something familiar—No. It was his eyes. His mind was playing tricks on him. *He had suffered too many hits*. But then the lead man stepped closer, removed his mask, and Vince Sweeney knew he wasn't dreaming. *Maybe he was dead*.

He had to be dead. There was no other way that he was seeing this.

The man reached out and touched Vince on the cheek.

"I'm sorry," Vince croaked. Slowly, the other men were lowering their masks too. Vince felt the worst sorrow he'd ever experienced, like the devil had reached into his chest and pulled out his heart, squeezing out his soul. "No, you can't be dead, too," he said to the other men.

"Vince, it's okay. You're going to be okay," the specter said.

Vince shook his head. "We're dead. We're all dead, and it's my fault." He was looking away now. He didn't want to see the images. He tried to push them away, but the man's hands stayed where they were before moving to his chin, lifting Vince's head to look him in the eye.

"Vince, it's okay. We're all here. We're all alive."

Could it really be? Could it?

"Mr. President?" Vince said, tears coming to his eyes. He'd fully expected death to take him, and his addled mind still didn't know if this was real. But he wanted to believe.

"It's me, Vince," President Zimmer said. "Let's get you out of this chair, okay?"

As soon as they released the straps, Vince's body fell limp. It wasn't the others in the room, Cal, Daniel, Gaucho or Trent, who was now holding him up. It was the president. *Why was he there?*

"Karl?" Vince asked.

"He's in rough shape, but we'll get him help."

Vince shook his head. He wanted to tell the president everything. He wanted to tell him that Karl was dying, and there was nothing they could do, that they were all helpless to save him. Then that special spark within him relit, the one that had sent him down to the recruiter's office, the one that had sent him through ranger training and into the most elite unit of all.

He was back in a flash. "Mr. President, I'm sorry. We should have been more careful."

The president looked at him with grave eyes and shook his head. "No Vince, I'm the one who should be sorry. It was my job. You and Karl were my responsibility." He got a better grip around Vince's waist as they headed out the door. "Now, how about we get you both home."

EPILOGUE

The place was more beautiful than Karl had described. The pictures Vince had seen didn't do the place justice. The little white cabin with the red tin roof was just the beginning of his amazement. The property spread over nearly 100 rolling acres. It used to be a boys' summer camp but sat vacant for years. The existing amenities included a small lake surrounded by plenty of trails, a couple of bunkhouses, and even an old cafeteria. It would take some work, but Vince and Karl were excited about seeing the first step in their dreams come true.

Vince bought the place sight unseen. Then Cal and Jonah Layton, CEO of The Jefferson Group, stepped in and pieced together an additional 2,000 acres of land surrounding the property. Vince was amazed at what vast amounts of money could buy. He truly felt blessed.

It had taken a week to wrap up the closing on the cabin property and another three for the other properties to be placed under contract. Those would close in the coming months. And so he'd come with Karl to the cabin, and for the

last five nights they'd finally gotten to call their dream property home.

Each morning shortly after rising, he made coffee for Karl
and himself. He then carried it to Karl's bedroom where Karl
lay with an IV bag stuck into his arm via long plastic tubes.
He was alert; he'd even regained every bit of his fiery nature.

That morning, Vince had already delivered the morning
coffee. He was just stepping outside to take a look at the
bunkhouses. He wanted to make a guesstimate on how many
months it would take to repair the buildings.

To his surprise, he saw a car coming up the drive. It was a
blue sedan that he didn't recognize, a rental probably. Maybe
the occupants were lost travelers or possibly campers revis-
iting the memories and the camp where they had stayed in
the cabins when young.

Vince was curious, so he stood on the side of the porch,
sipping his coffee, waiting for the blue sedan to arrive. It
parked next to the big oak tree with a single rope dangling
from an enormous limb that Karl assumed had at one time
held a tire swing.

Two men stepped out. Instantly, Vince knew they were
Secret Service.

"Mr. Sweeney?" one of them queried.

"That's me."

"We were sent to take a look around this property. Is now
a good time?"

"Be my guest."

He'd expected something like this. Maybe it was something the Secret Service always did in case the president was
ever to visit an old friend. *They must just be getting the lay of the
land*, Vince thought.

The men returned fifteen minutes later during which time
Vince had already gotten himself a second cup of coffee.

"Thank you for your time, sir," said one of the agents

before slipping back into the car. No other words were offered before the blue sedan was executing a three-point turn, heading back down the gravel drive.

No matter how long Vince had been in contact with the United States Government, he never quite got used to how focused on expediting their duties most of them were, often at the expense of appearing brusque. He would have been happy to offer the lads a strong mug of coffee and most likely a bite to eat if they had stuck around.

Oh well. There were things to do. He put the brief visit out of his mind, and crossed the dirt road to tackle his morning tasks.

Soon a series of honks sounded down the drive. Vince reflexively reached for his sidearm, pulling it from his waistband. One, then two, then three more heavy-duty trucks came into view, all pulling trailers packed with stacks of lumber - piles and piles of wood and bags of cement. As the trucks got closer, he saw Gaucho driving the lead vehicle, but who was in the passenger seat?

My God, that's the president. What's he doing here?

Once the vehicles were parked, the men started piling out. The sheer number of men reminded Vince of ants carrying food away from a picnic table. Accompanying Gaucho and the president were MSgt Willy Trent, Cal Stokes, the sniper Daniel Briggs, the portly gentleman, Dr. Higgins and young Neil Patel. Prancing along like she owned the place was the dog. What was her name? Ah, Liberty! Vince remembered she'd been a present from Cal's deceased cousin, Travis Hayden.

Two more familiar faces stepped out, and Vince had to swallow the lump in his throat. It was Christian and his grandfather. Christian ran to him, wrapping his arms around Vince's waist. "This place is awesome, Vince. Have you gone in the lake yet?"

"Not yet, buddy," Vince said with a chuckle, truly happy to see the young man.

Everyone was gathered together in an extraordinary show of support, and Vince had difficulty keeping his emotions in check. "I don't understand. Why are you guys here? Mr. President, shouldn't you be—"

"We wanted to be here. We want to be with Karl."

Vince had been the one to provide an update to President Brandon Zimmer. The best doctors said Karl had days, maybe weeks. Despite his outward optimism, Karl's body was finally submitting to the cancer that had spread to almost every inch of his body. The IV fluids were the only things keeping life manageable, with a heavy dose of pain medication on constant drip.

"What's all that?" Vince asked, pointing to the trucks.

Gaucho grinned. "I talked to Karl. He said you guys might need a little help getting this place back in working shape. We made a couple of calls, and here we are to get this place shipshape. Consider us the most elite working party you've ever had at your disposal."

That's when Vince noticed they were all dressed in working clothes. The president pulled a pair of work gloves out of his back pocket. "I'm going to go say hi to Karl, and after that, how about you tell us where we can get started?"

———

Cal threw the tennis ball into the lake as far as he could, prompting Liberty to take a sprinting jump to fetch the projectile. She swam, legs pumping furiously while everyone laughed from the sandy beach.

They had made a lot of progress in the past three days. It turned out Karl had done a stint with the Navy Seabees while stationed in Guam. Along with the summers working construction as a kid, he was the resident expert when it came to repairing and rebuilding.

While he didn't have the strength to pick up a hammer, he directed it all from the sidelines. In the way of a man accustomed to living a hard life, Karl was happy to be with the others, executing orders and staying busy. There were only a couple of times Cal had seen Karl's face turn melancholy, like he realized he would never be the one swinging the hammer again.

By the end of three days, they'd not only repaired the holes in the bunkroom roofs, thrown out all the old cots and replaced them with new ones, but they'd also built a 1,000-meter rifle range and a long row of pistol pits. There was still plenty of work to do, but they could see the fruits of their labor.

They'd spent their days digging, cutting and hammering away. Top was skillfully moving tons of dirt with the front loader they rented, and Dr. Higgins was particularly talented using the electric saw.

Each day, everyone gathered to eat lunch together by the lake. Conversations only ceased when Liberty took time to entertain the men by fetching balls in the water, or chasing a bird or squirrel that had gotten too close to the action.

Night times were especially memorable as the men sat gathered around the campfire. Everyone chipped in, relating their stories. Even Christian's grandfather opened up, telling of his days in the Djibouti Army.

The men had gathered to make light work of the property's projects, but especially to be with Karl in his last days. They'd come to be together, but they'd come for a fellow warrior—to spend those last precious days together and see him off.

Back in the real world, America was clamoring to hear from their resurrected president. Zimmer had turned into an overnight sensation. Everyone wanted to see him, to make sure he was really alive. He'd told the men staying at the new property about how he'd escaped, aided in no small way by Elliot Peabody and his impressive Djibouti spy ring. It had been Peabody who'd tipped off the president about General Hachi's assassination scheme. After that it was just a matter of coordinating a good old fashioned switcheroo where the plane had stopped just long enough behind the airport hangar for the two presidents and their security to jump out and hide. The plane had taken off by remote control, with the cost of the lost plane a small price to pay to uncover the truth.

But even though the president could have jumped to the mic, he instead avoided the spotlight, choosing to stay among his friends. He kept his promise, only occasionally taking phone calls that he knew he couldn't avoid. Cal had asked him that first day about the status of the presidential election and how the recent events in Djibouti might change things. Zimmer had looked at him cautiously, like he was still trying to make a decision that he wasn't yet ready to share. Cal picked up on the hint, and he never broached the subject again. Politics wasn't his business anyway, and there was plenty of real work to do.

Once the repairs were complete, he and Zimmer would make sure private and federal agencies were the first to hear about Vince and Karl's new venture. There would be plenty of time for that. Right now, they would enjoy each other's company during a hard day's work and spend the nights reliving the past and making dreams for their futures.

———

The helicopter touched down in the grassy clearing. Congressman Tony McKnight waited until the pilot told him it was okay to step out. He could see the president waiting at the far end of the clearing. His stomach turned. He didn't know why he'd been summoned and, truth be told, he wondered if there were snipers hidden deep in the woods. Maybe the president had lured him there to execute him.

He tried to remind himself that the Chinese were the only ones who knew about McKnight's involvement in the incidents that unfolded in Djibouti. The warning was clear: keep your mouth shut, and we'll be in touch. Still, he couldn't shake the feeling that he was being watched. There had been more than a couple of occasions in the preceding weeks when he'd spotted an onlooker who seemed out of place at a primary stop.

After receiving the package with his moneyman's head, he'd almost panicked. Almost. Disposing of the head hadn't been easy, but he had his ways. For a solid eighteen hours, twelve minutes, and three seconds, he'd considered dropping out of the race. There was President Brandon Zimmer to consider, and there was also a chance the Chinese might say something.

As the days passed, that became less and less likely. There'd been reports from China that Vice Premier Wang Ling had died in his sleep while on a trip to Hong Kong. That could not have been a coincidence, and it served as a further warning to him.

So here it was, possibly the final confrontation with President Zimmer. The congressman tried to steady his legs as he stepped out of the helicopter and started to make his way across the field. The president was dressed in what McKnight considered outdoor gear: heavy work boots, blue jeans, and a T-shirt. There was no Secret Service to be seen. The helicopter lifted off once again, buffeting him with the downdraft.

Still, President Zimmer stood there waiting, his face

completely unreadable. Tony wondered whether he could have killed the president if he had a weapon. No, that was just silly. There was no way someone wasn't watching. As soon as the idea came into his head, he kicked it away, and he continued walking.

McKnight had no idea where he was. They hadn't told him, and it wasn't like he carried a GPS around. They'd even taken his phone from him before lifting off. When the president summoned you immediately answered his bid. It was better to face the fire than to cower in the shadows.

He'd never seen Brandon with what looked like a full week's worth of stubble on his face. Zimmer appeared to be in his element, whereas McKnight was still clothed in a full suit and tie. The president seemed preoccupied, though. He must've been making some kind of decision in his head as McKnight stepped closer, finally within arm's reach. Then, the congressman realized the president was wearing earbuds.

Zimmer pressed a finger to his left ear and said, "Sorry, I was just listening to a little work music. I can't tell you the last time I had time to listen to music by myself. Must be the outdoors." The president chuckled and looked like his usual self. He reached out his hand, "Sorry to call you out here on such short notice, Tony."

"I live to serve at your pleasure, Mr. President," McKnight said, flashing what he hoped was a convincing confident smile.

"I assume my people have already briefed you on what I wished to talk about."

"No, Mr. President. They didn't say anything. They just told me where to be and that I might be gone a couple of hours."

The president smacked a work glove on his thigh. "Damn. Thought I'd sent them that email—maybe I didn't—Hell, I don't know. This simple life - you should try it sometime,

Tony. I've got to say, it sure has a way of clearing your head. Anyway, down to business."

Here it comes, he thought, although Brandon seemed a little too at ease considering what he was about to do, but perhaps Zimmer was more ruthless than he had ever imagined possible. Either way, the congressman wouldn't back down.

"Tony, I just wanted to thank you for everything you said when everything went down in Djibouti. I can't tell you how much it means, especially during an election year. I saw what some of our other friends were saying, and frankly, I would have thought that you would have picked up the 'Zimmer is an idiot' banner, too."

My God! Did he just bring me here to express his gratitude?

Relief flooded through McKnight's body like the hallowed touch of an angel. It was everything he could do to keep his legs from buckling.

"Mr. President, I just did what I thought was right."

"I'm glad to see that you and I have that in common, Tony. Despite what happens in the coming months, I really hope we can continue to work together, facing the challenges our country must resolve. I value your friendship and our strong working relationship."

"I share your sentiments, sir."

"The political arena has a funny way of testing men's fortitude and character. I've lost some very good friends because they turned out to be liars and cheats. They'd present one image to the public, but live a completely different life in private. It sickens me sometimes. And I'll tell you, I'm not embarrassed to say that there was a point where I thought I might not seek reelection." Zimmer gestured to the woods all around him, to the Smoky Mountains in the distance.

"It would be easier to come out to a place like this and live peacefully the remainder of my days. I would turn off the news, put on some headphones, and listen to some old

country music while building something I could be proud of."
The president paused as if considering that option seriously.
Then, he looked back at McKnight and said, "But the world
needs men like us, Tony. We have decided to put our lives on
hold in order to make this country, this world, better. I will
fight tooth and nail to make sure that I've done the best job I
can." He exhaled, ending his sermon. "Well, anyway, it's
something to think about, but for now, why don't you come
join us for lunch? I'd like to introduce you to some of my
friends."

––––––––––

Two days later, Vince walked into Karl's room to deliver his
morning coffee. He set the cup down and nudged his friend's
shoulder. Karl's eyes fluttered open. It took him a moment to
realize that Vince was there. There was something different
in Karl's eyes, not a look of vacancy, but something close, and
that was when Vince knew. "I'll be right back, okay?" he said
to his friend. Karl didn't nod, but continued to stare with that
empty look.

Everybody else was gathered downstairs eating breakfast
in the kitchen. A hush fell over the room as they saw Vince's
face when he entered the room.

"It's time," Vince said simply. None of them said a word,
just got up from their chairs and followed Vince upstairs.

Karl was still breathing, but now his eyes were closed. He
was focusing on that one last task, that one last test of
strength before his body gave way. The king-sized bed had
been moved to the middle of the room to make room for all
the medical equipment. Vince saw Dr. Higgins increase the
pain medication upon entering the room.

After they had all found spots around the bed, Vince
reached under the mattress. He pulled out a full bottle of

Jack Daniels, opened it, raised it in the air, and said, "To Karl."

Everybody repeated in unison, "To Karl."

Vince took a swig and then passed the bottle around, first to the president and then it was passed to Cal, Daniel, Gaucho, Trent, Dr. Higgins, Neil, Christian, the grandfather, and then back to Vince. He replaced the top, and placed the bottle in the crook of Karl's arm.

All the words had already been said. They'd enjoyed their time, Karl probably the most. There had been visitors along the way, including friends from the Army who stopped in to pay their respects. There would definitely be more when they held the funeral, but for now, it was just these men.

There, in the cabin with a red tin roof, the grandfather reached out a hand and placed it on Karl. Daniel followed suit, and soon, they all reached out to touch the dying warrior. There they stood, waiting, until finally Dr. Higgins gave Vince a nod to signal that Karl had died.

In that moment, Vince stopped fighting back the tears. Of course he was sad for his friend. He would miss Karl more than he'd ever missed anyone, but he cried because he was happy beyond measure that Karl's last days had been spent with fellow warriors who had been more than willing to put everything else aside to help escort him into the valley of death. Colonel Vince Sweeney looked around the room, smiled, and hoped that one day he might be so lucky.

———

I hope you enjoyed this story.

If you did, please take a moment to write a review ON AMAZON. Even the short ones help!

GET A FREE COPY OF THE CORPS JUSTICE

PREQUEL SHORT STORY, *GOD-SPEED*, JUST FOR SUBSCRIBING AT <u>CG-COOPER.COM</u>

MORE THANKS TO MY BETA READERS:

Marry, Don, Sue, Judith, Paul, Susan, Wanda, Phil, Craig, Doug and David. Thanks for keeping me honest.

ALSO BY C. G. COOPER

The Corps Justice Series In Order:

Back To War

Council Of Patriots

Prime Asset

Presidential Shift

National Burden

Lethal Misconduct

Moral Imperative

Disavowed

Chain Of Command

Papal Justice

The Zimmer Doctrine

Sabotage

Liberty Down

Sins Of The Father

Corps Justice Short Stories:

Chosen

God-Speed

Running

The Daniel Briggs Novels:

Adrift

Fallen

Broken

Tested

The Tom Greer Novels

A Life Worth Taking

The Spy In Residence Novels

What Lies Hidden

The Alex Knight Novels:

Breakout

The Stars & Spies Series:

Backdrop

The Patriot Protocol Series:

The Patriot Protocol

The Chronicles of Benjamin Dragon:

Benjamin Dragon – Awakening

Benjamin Dragon – Legacy

Benjamin Dragon - Genesis

ABOUT THE AUTHOR

C. G. Cooper is the *USA TODAY* and AMAZON BESTSELLING author of the CORPS JUSTICE novels (including spinoffs), The Chronicles of Benjamin Dragon and the Patriot Protocol series.

Cooper grew up in a Navy family and traveled from one Naval base to another as he fed his love of books and a fledgling desire to write.

Upon graduating from the University of Virginia with a degree in Foreign Affairs, Cooper was commissioned in the

United States Marine Corps and went on to serve six years as an infantry officer. C. G. Cooper's final Marine duty station was in Nashville, Tennessee, where he fell in love with the laid-back lifestyle of Music City.

His first published novel, BACK TO WAR, came out of a need to link back to his time in the Marine Corps. That novel, written as a side project, spawned many follow-on novels, several exciting spinoffs, and catapulted Cooper's career.

Cooper lives just south of Nashville with his wife, three children, and their German shorthaired pointer, Liberty, who's become a popular character in the Corps Justice novels.

When he's not writing or hosting his podcast, Books In 30, Cooper spends time with his family, does his best to improve his golf handicap, and loves to shed light on the ongoing fight of everyday heroes.

Cooper loves hearing from readers and responds to every email personally.

To connect with C. G. Cooper visit
www.cg-cooper.com

Made in the USA
Middletown, DE
10 September 2020